Getting Rid of Karenna

Other books by Helena Pielichaty

Vicious Circle
Simone's Letters

Getting Rid of Karenna

Helena Pielichaty

OXFORD
UNIVERSITY PRESS

OXFORD

UNIVERSITY PRESS

Great Clarendon Street, Oxford OX2 6DP

Oxford University Press is a department of the University of Oxford.
It furthers the University's objective of excellence in research, scholarship,
and education by publishing worldwide in

Oxford New York

Athens Auckland Bangkok Bogotá Buenos Aires Calcutta
Cape Town Chennai Dar es Salaam Delhi Florence Hong Kong Istanbul
Karachi Kuala Lumpur Madrid Melbourne Mexico City Mumbai
Nairobi Paris São Paulo Singapore Taipei Tokyo Toronto Warsaw

and associated companies in Berlin Ibadan

Oxford is a registered trade mark of Oxford University Press
in the UK and in certain other countries

British Library Cataloguing in Publication Data available

ISBN 0 19 271819 3

Typeset by AFS Image Setters Ltd, Glasgow
Printed and bound in Great Britain by Biddles Ltd, www.Biddles.co.uk

Dedicated to:
Naomi Anna Dworski
who died young and stayed pretty
6 April 1983 – 8 November 1996

1

I awoke with James Dean smiling down at me. 'Good morning, Deany,' I said to his shiny, poster face, 'sleep well?' He gave me his brief-but-sexy nod. 'Sure, Suzanne. I always sleep well in your bedroom.'

'Stop it,' I murmured, 'you're making me blush!'

I know it's sad fancying someone who's been dead nearly fifty years but, as boyfriends go, Jimmy D. is perfect: easy to talk to, never critical, and always there when you needed him. Unlike in the real world.

For a moment, I wondered why I was awake. My alarm read 6.45 a.m. I didn't do a.m.s at weekends. Annoyed, I turned over to go back to sleep, when there was a knock on the door. 'Are you decent?' Dad asked, before walking straight in, closely followed by Sam, my five-year-old brother, who leaped on top of me.

'Wakey, wakey, sweetheart!' he yelled.

Groaning, I pushed his soft, fat feet out of my face. 'Go away,' I mumbled, slowly remembering the reason for the early call.

Sam giggled, wrapping his arms around my neck. As usual, he smelt lovely, like fresh bread. Dad slid a mug of tea on to my bedside cabinet and lifted Sammy away. 'Aww!' we chorused. Little bro wriggled in protest, losing one of his Hercules slippers. 'I want to stay in bed with Suzanne. She doesn't do smelly ones like Chris.'

Dad chose to ignore this sad-but-true fact about his nineteen-year-old first-born with whom Sam shared a bedroom. 'Not today. Suzanne's getting up now. She's starting work as a Saturday girl this fine, February morning.'

'Assistant,' I grumbled, 'Saturday assistant.' This was a difficult household to convert to political correctness. He'd call me princess in a minute.

'Assistant,' Dad amended. 'Your sister is going to go out into the world of capitalism to supplement the meagre thruppence ha'penny she gets from us.'

This is a dig at me. As a former inhabitant of planet Days-gone-by, Geoffrey Fish thinks I still play netball for Year Six and need only 20p a week for sweets and a *Beano*.

'Better get a move on, princess, you don't want to be late on your first day.'

I readjusted my pillows. 'I've got ages yet. Don't start till half-eight.'

'Where've I heard that one before?' he asked, leading Sam out.

'Is the bathroom free?' I called after him.

'There was no charge last time I looked!'

Ah, fathers and their little jokes. Every one a gem.

Downstairs, the menu choice for vegetarians entering the labour market was waffles and Mr Men pasta shapes. 'I'm not hungry, Dad, honest,' I protested but Dad just pointed to the breakfast bar and I sat, like the obedient middle child I am. My parents are so lucky.

Reluctantly, I chewed on Misters Happy and Tall. I was beginning to feel nervous about this job. I hadn't even been into Snippits, the hair salon where I was starting, although I passed it every day on the bus journey to school. Everything had been sorted out on the phone two days ago when, on the off-chance and desperate for cash, I answered an ad in the free newspaper. Tina Lockwood, the manageress, just seemed relieved that I could start straight away. 'Shampoo and sweep, love, that's all I need you to do,' she had said in a deep, raspy voice. Shampoo and sweep. I could manage that, couldn't I?

Dad fussed around me as I got ready to leave, handing me my Sheffield United scarf and unexpectedly pressing four quid into my hand. 'Remember what I told you about your hours, Suzanne. Eight maximum and an hour's break in between; that's the law for sixteen year olds.'

'I know! I know! It's a only a hairdresser's, Dad. There's no chimney climbing involved.'

'Never mind chimneys. I know what some of these bosses get up to, especially with young kids.'

Dad had been union rep down at the steel works before he was made redundant six years ago and it still showed.

I tried to reassure him, knowing he was worried about me. 'Father, dearest, I know there's no such thing as tartan paint and if they tell me to go for a long stand I'll reply that the old ones are always the best. Panic not!'

'God give me chance,' he smiled.

'What about you, are you working today, comrade?' I asked.

Dad ran his fingers through his thick, brown hair and looked crumpled. I knew his upholstery business wasn't doing too well—I'd heard Mum on the phone to Auntie Jan about it. He shrugged. 'Erm, if I can fix the van then I've got one or two estimates to go to in Firth Park.'

'Can I come?' Sam asked, wiping tomato sauce from his chin in preparation.

'If you're good.'

Sam opened his eyes innocent-wide. 'I'm always good.'

I bent down to kiss the little cherub, already missing him. 'See you tonight, tiger. Lyndsay's coming round so make sure you're looking cool.'

His face lit up. He knew he couldn't marry me so he'd cottoned on to the next best thing—his adored sister's best mate. 'I will. I'll wear my new trainers. Is she still going out with yukky Jez?'

' 'Fraid so, Sam, but she'll soon change her mind when she sees those Velcro straps. Tell you what, why don't you go and pull Christian's duvet off? You know he likes that.'

'OK.'

Little bro raced off and I called to Dad in the kitchen to tell him I was going. 'Say hi to Mum for me when she comes in,' I added. Mum was a midwife at the Infirmary. She was on nights and hadn't arrived back yet.

'I will,' Dad promised, following me out as far as his 'van', a converted ambulance we called Old Bluey which blocked the whole driveway. 'And a bucket of steam,' he grinned, 'don't fall for it if they ask you to fetch a bucket of steam!'

My breath puffed out in thick, cold clouds as, having avoided all the sparkly frozen dog turds, I reached the bottom of our road and the crest of Roman Hill. I don't know which bright geezer decided to build an estate on top of one of Sheffield's seven hills but I know he never had to live here in winter. Still, the views were brilliant, for those who made it.

At the foot of Roman Hill our uninspiring semi-detached houses gave way to a few remaining Victorian terraces before widening out to the council estate.

Winding my scarf more tightly round my neck I crossed over Pike Street and on to Portland Street where the early Saturday morning traffic was already stressing-out the tarmac.

'The Piazza' was a concrete-grey row of small shops sandwiched between The Bricklayers Arms to the left and a garage on the right. Jason's Fish Bar, a bakery, a bookies, The Wash Tub launderette and, last but not least, Snippits Unisex Hair Salon made up the rest. I had arrived at work.

4

I had arrived at work but no one else had. Snippits remained dark and slightly intimidating. I peered through the window, careful to side-step a splattering of regurgitated tikka marsala near the doorway. Inside, I could just make out the domed shapes of antiquated hairdryers, draped in towels like a row of defeated boxers. I checked my watch: 8:15.

'Tina's always late, even though she only lives in the flat above,' a voice chimed next to me. 'You the new Saturday lass? Suzanne?'

Twisting round, I fixed on my eager-to-please smile and nodded. A tired-looking woman with a blotchy red face gazed at me with mild curiosity. She shrugged from inside her thin jacket, either at me or the cold, or both. 'I'm Candy,' she said. I thought of dry Turkish delight left over from Christmas. 'I work here part-time. Used to be full-time but when I had our Soroya I said I only wanted part-time. No point having babies if you're not there to look after them, is there?'

'I suppose not,' I agreed.

'Scott's looking after her today. He's her dad—we're not married, we live together, like. My mum has her mid-week. Can't be doing with childminders. Did you read about that one who battered that baby's head against a wall? Disgusting. They want to have the same thing done to them in my opinion. You still at school?'

I blinked at the sudden change in subject. 'Yes.'

'Which one?'

'Steetley.'

'Steetley? That's dead rough, in't it?'

It was my turn to shrug. 'It's getting better.'

'I wouldn't send my kids there.'

'Wouldn't you?'

'They have bullying, don't they?'

'It's optional after Year Nine,' I said flippantly, though it was true. Steetley High School was near the bottom of the league tables, the Norway of the Eurovision Song Contest.

Candy sniffed, her mouth curling into a near-smile. '"Optional after Year Nine". Very good. Very funny. You'll fit in well here, you will. Don't make me laugh too much, though, cos I can't hold owt in since I had our Soroya. She was a right big baby. Doctor said to me "This one's ready for school!" when she pulled her out. Nine pounds eleven.'

'That is big,' I acknowledged. I wasn't a midwife's daughter for nothing.

'Tell you what, though, I love her to bits but they're hard work. Don't have a baby till you're ready; that's my advice. Got a boyfriend, have you?'

I thought of Lee Anderson leaning close to me in chemistry yesterday. 'No,' I replied wistfully.

Keys rattled from inside the shop. 'She's here,' Candy informed me in a loud whisper. 'She's nice is Tina. Good to work for, but you'll have to watch Karenna, the junior stylist. She's all right sometimes but catch her on a bad day—moody or what?'

'Karenna?' I asked, my mouth going dry instantly.

Candy nodded absently as we waited for the manageress to undo the bolts. 'Mmm. Karenna Sheldon. Lives up Wincobank. Do you know her?'

I dug my hands deep into my coat pockets, feeling dizzy and sick. Oh, I knew Karenna all right.

Tina smiled, first at Candy, then more broadly at me as we walked through the door, her crayoned eyebrows lifting like two railway arches as she quickly looked me up and down. 'Aren't you lovely and tall?' she exclaimed. 'Isn't she lovely and tall?' she called to Candy, who had disappeared through a louvred door at the back of the shop. Candy re-emerged, coatless and nodding in agreement.

'Yes. I noticed that.'

My arm was grabbed in what I supposed was a friendly gesture and I was escorted to the nearby kidney-shaped reception desk. Here, Tina reached out with her free hand and fumbled for a worn black book; her bleached nail scoring a line down the side of a scrawled-over page. 'Marvellous. I've no one until Mrs Venn at 8.45, so we can snatch ten minutes. You go through to the staffroom and put the kettle on while I have a word with Candy about rotas.'

Fortunately, the staffroom was empty and I breathed a sigh of relief. She wasn't here yet. In fact, she wasn't coming at all. Couldn't be. I'd misheard what Candy had said because I was nervous about starting work. I got like that sometimes—over-anxious; jumpy, thinking people had said one thing when they'd said another. Positive thoughts only, Suzanne. Candy hadn't said 'Karenna Sheldon' she'd said 'Karen had her shelf done' or something.

I searched for a kettle. The staffroom was really a cupboard, separated from the rest of the shop by thin teak-effect cladding. Opposite a pair of black leatherette chairs protruded a stainless steel sink with a water heater above it and a tarnished mirror nearby. I couldn't see a kettle or signs of coffee.

I noticed another door next to the chairs. Thinking this was a storeroom I pushed into a darkened recess only to have the door swing back with a bang. 'Wait your turn!' a voice rang out.

It was then my life fell apart.

So she was here—and on the bog. How ironic can you get? I just stood there, rigid, staring at the closed door in this dim back room, waiting for Her to appear, then to stare and smile and start again.

7

2

The lavatory flushed and out she came: Karenna Sheldon, junior stylist and ace-sadist. I glanced furtively at her, to confirm the worst—that it was the real thing who hadn't, after all, died the brutal, long death I had prayed for so many times.

Sheldon had always been pretty, but she wasn't pretty any more—she was fantastic. Even in this half-light I could see that. Her natural fair hair was expertly styled into a French plait, exposing her flawless skin and high cheekbones. A stylish, short, black dress clung to her narrow waist making her look elegant and sophisticated and miles older than nineteen. Although I was taller, I felt instantly too ugly and too scruffy next to her.

She rinsed her hands briefly under the cold water tap at the sink and glanced at me over her shoulder. 'You the new girl?' she asked.

My throat was still dry. I swallowed, nodding like an idiot. She headed out towards the salon. 'Well, I hope you're better than the last one we had.' At the doorway she paused, looking straight at me. 'What are you meant to be doing?'

'Coffee.'

'Down there, under the sink. I'll have mine black today. I stayed here with Tina last night—made the mistake of trying to keep up with her on gin. My head's killing—serves me right.'

'Where's the kettle?' I stammered, hardly believing I could ask such a normal question.

She pointed to the boiler. 'That thing is the kettle. Watch when it drips, though—you could burn yourself.'

'Oh.'

'Get on with it then, dozy. I've got Mrs Pearson any minute.'

'Oh, sure.'

I stooped to open the cupboard, which smelt of damp and Domestos. There was a catering tin of Nescafé on a tray along with half a bag of sugar and a jar of whitener. With shaking hands, I lifted the tray on to the draining board and began my task, realizing that she had not recognized me.

Well, if she didn't recognize me, I certainly wasn't going to remind her. Wasn't going to say, 'Hey, girl, do you remember me? Suzanne? Suzanne Fish—you know—the skinny kid you terrified, oh, it must be five years ago now? Me, the timid little new girl against you, Fiona Featherstone, and that Jamillah Ahmed—all two years older. Bit unfair, those odds, when I come to think about it—and I do still think about it, Karenna. Now, do you take sugar or are you sweet enough?'

With trembling hands I spooned coffee into three cups, praying the flashbacks wouldn't begin again and wondering how I would get through the day. Fortunately Tina provided the perfect solution, her voice apologetic but direct.

'Leave those a minute, love. I've just seen that mess on the shop front. You'll have to get a mop and clean it up. No one else is free.'

Gladly, I scrubbed and swilled the vomit I had daintily avoided earlier, wondering vaguely where curry-clearance came in my job description but reasoning I'd rather do that than stand next to Sheldon. Karenna Sheldon! God! Of all the people!

I was tempted to run home but I was too much of a coward to be a coward. No change there then. What would I say to Dad for starters? Sorry, Geoff, couldn't stick it—met this lass who bullied me for two years.

What? What lass who bullied me? I forgot to mention it?
Well . . .

Besides, I argued to myself as I tipped the slops down
the drain, I wasn't a kid any more and she hadn't
recognized me. I'd be fine.

Psychiatrists call it denial.

The rest of the morning passed surprisingly quickly. I
shampooed two clients without drowning them and
made coffees for two others without poisoning them. I
assisted Tina with a perm and fetched magazines for
Candy's 'lady'.

Even though she was the busiest, Karenna didn't ask
me to do anything. She seemed to prefer to work
independently, chatting smoothly to her clients and
smiling regally as they inevitably slid a tip into her hand
afterwards, unaware of my constant spying.

After lunch I was asked to help Candy again. I
decided I liked Candy; she reminded me of my
grandma. She had strong opinions about everything
and didn't mind who knew it. Having covered
compulsory question a) for hairdressers: 'Is it still cold
out?' with her client, Mrs Spennimore, Candy had
moved on to compulsory question b) 'Are you going
anywhere special tonight?'

Mrs Spennimore, a small, cuddly woman who had
overdone it with the body spray, beamed beneath her
newly-washed-about-to-be-permed mop. 'It's my silver
wedding anniversary "do" tonight.'

Candy gripped the woman's shoulder, her mouth fully
opened as if she'd just been left all her money in her
will. 'Fantastic! How many're coming?' she trilled.

'Thirty or forty. We didn't want to go overboard. Our
Gemma's coming home from America. She's bringing a
friend.'

'Is she? That's fantastic!' Candy held out her hand for
a blue curler and winked at me. 'Gemma's Mrs

10

Spennimore's daughter. She's a teacher. Where is it she's at?'

'Mansfield, Texas.'

'That's it. Is her friend a teacher, too?'

Mrs Spennimore's ears flamed crimson instantly. 'Yes,' she said, managing to heap the short word high with disapproval. 'Yes. And she's . . . hmm . . . she's gay!' she revealed.

'Oh,' Candy said shortly followed by, 'Pink one, Suzanne.'

'Not that Gemma is,' Mrs Spennimore added hastily. 'They're just good friends.'

'Well, I'm sorry, Greta, but I do not approve of that,' Candy announced, her mouth now set in a firm line.

'What?' Mrs Spennimore asked timidly.

'Lesbian teachers. I wouldn't want my Soroya taught by one. You wouldn't want to be taught by a lesbian, would you, Suzanne?'

I wanted to say that I couldn't care less, as long as they were good at their job, but I sensed that would be a Wrong Answer. I hesitated. 'Erm . . . '

'Although women PE teachers are often gay, of course,' Candy continued.

'Not mine,' Karenna interrupted, unexpectedly joining in, 'she was a real man-eater. Miss Kendall they called her.'

'She died,' I said, without thinking, 'she died last year.'

'What of?' Candy asked.

'Cancer,' I replied, aware Karenna was staring at me.

'Oh, now don't get me started on cancer,' Candy said, reaching for the packet of cotton wool. 'Half my family have died of cancer and the other half have had heart attacks.' She pulled out a length of cotton wool, rolling it into a long narrow strip which she then wedged around Mrs Spennimore's hairline. 'I wouldn't wish cancer on my worst enemy.'

11

'Which school do you go to?' Karenna asked casually, brushing stray hair from the back of her for-once vacant chair.

'Erm . . . Steetley,' I answered, eyes glued on the trolley of curlers in front of me. My heart began to beat faster. What did I have to open my big mouth for?

Candy pointed to a plastic hood which I handed to her with trembling fingers. 'I told Suzanne earlier on, there's no way I'd send any kid of mine to Steetley with the things they get up to there,' she informed us.

'I went to Steetley for a while. It was all right,' Karenna disclosed.

'Did you? I thought you went to Park High,' Candy said, glancing briefly at her colleague. Karenna shrugged.

'We moved halfway through.'

'Oh.'

Mrs Spennimore reached for her handbag and fumbled for a tube of mints. 'Gemma's never mixed with gay people before, not even when she went to Brighton for summer work. I don't understand it.'

For the rest of the afternoon I could almost hear the cogs in Karenna's brain turning round and round as she stole glances at me, connecting my name to my age to Steetley and finally to her. I was just taking an empty coffee cup away from her last client when she suddenly reached out and prodded me on the shoulder with a hairbrush. 'It's Suzanne Fish, isn't it? I remember you!'

She smiled widely in fake astonishment, as if conjuring up happy memories.

I glanced at her timidly. 'I remember you, too,' I mumbled, darting straight into the staffroom like a mouse into its hole.

3

I caught the bus home, staring bleakly through the grimy window, forcing Karenna Sheldon out of my thoughts. Go away, I willed her, go away. It's Saturday; I've got a mate coming round—we're going to swap CDs and talk about sex—so you can see I've no room for you in my brain, perm-woman. Go away, I willed again, go away.

It didn't work; Karenna's smiling face replacing my gaunt reflection in the glass. Stay then, I challenged. You can't touch me now; I'm a Year Eleven, doing really well, despite you always calling me a 'spaz'. And I'm a Star Mentor—you wouldn't know about our mentoring system at Steetley. It started after you left. We have a new head now—Mrs Parminter—she's great. You wouldn't have got away with half of what you did if she'd been there five years ago, no matter how far out you'd thrust your B cups at the male teachers, you daft tart.

I smiled and her image faded. That was better. I'd always been an expert at slagging Sheldon off; in my head at least.

Chris was waiting at the terminus as I stepped off the bus, towering above everyone else in the queue. Tall, yes, lovely, no. 'Hail, sister,' he greeted.

'Hail, loser,' I replied mechanically.

'You lasted a full day, then?' he said.

'Just about.'

13

'Lend me ten quid.'

'Yeah, right, giving you my money was exactly what I had planned for it. Where are you going so early, anyway?'

He beat his chest, warrior-like. 'Town to drink heartily with the mighty men of Hillsborough, then on to some wenching at the noble Sarah's.'

'She still doesn't know you're gay, then?'

I always allowed myself to be un-PC with Chris. It was the only way of getting through.

'Such wit wasted on one so plain,' he retorted, ducking on to the platform as the bus began to pull away.

'Funny boy!' I yelled into the diesel fumes. Slowly, I trudged home, grateful that at least Lynz and I would be free from him taking the rip out of us tonight.

I shrugged off my jacket and draped it over the banister. I was back, in my safe place. Nothing had changed: the hallway still needed decorating, my school bag was still under the telephone table where I'd chucked it yesterday, my family still loved me, and Wednesday were still crap. I could relax now.

Sam, the nice brother, charged through, hugging my legs. 'Did you have a cool time?' he asked.

'So-so. How about you? Were you good?'

He nodded, trailing into the living room. 'I was very good. A fat lady gave me 10p and some malt loaf and said I was "a little love".'

'Mega.'

Taking a deep breath, I went into the kitchen and prepared to relive my day, or a diluted version of it. Just like in the past when Karenna had given me a hard time at school and I'd come in and pretend I had nothing worse on my mind than too much geography homework. I was unnerved by how quickly I seemed to be reverting.

Mum was browsing through the paper, looking cosy in her dressing gown while Dad attacked something on the cooker with a spatula. They both smiled warmly at me. 'How did it go?' Mum enquired.

'OK.'

'Talk about the weather a lot?'

'Yep.'

'Knew it.' She handed me a mug of tea.

'Any long stands, then?' Dad asked cheerfully.

'What's for dinner?' I asked, deliberately changing the subject.

'Spag bol.'

'And for me?' the awkward vegetarian of the family asked.

'Dry bread and pull-it,' Mum teased.

'Don't. I'm not in the mood,' I replied sullenly. 'I'm getting changed.'

'Dinner in ten minutes, Suze,' Dad called after me.

Upstairs, I changed quickly, forcing myself to plan ahead rather than dwell on events at Snippits. I'd have a bath straight after dinner, then chill out with Lynz before ending the evening by arguing about footy with Dad during *Match of the Day*. Perfect. There's a lot to be said for denial. I highly recommend it.

When I returned downstairs, Chris, thankfully, was now Main Topic. It was all the usual stuff—he was never in, he'd fail his A level re-sits again this year if he didn't buckle down and why did he want to go to Nottingham University just because that's where Sarah was going? Didn't the boy have a mind of his own? 'Robin Hood lives in Nottingham,' Sam said, interrupting the flow.

'Yes, he does,' Mum replied, side-tracked.

'Can we see him when we visit Chris?'

'Not the real Robin Hood, he's dead.'

'How did he die?'

Mum frowned. 'I don't know, actually. You'll have to ask Suzanne—she's the brain-box.'

Here we go. Let the labelling commence. At school I was either Brain Woman or Boff Girl or Swotty Git or some other equally original title. This is what comes of being only one of three pupils in the entire history of Steetley to take maths GCSE a year early.

'My daughter, the genius,' Dad smiled proudly, adding his own.

If only he knew.

Mum pulled at my arm to read my watch. 'Better get ready, I suppose. Only one more night shift to do then three days of bliss.' I was treated to a quick, annoying ruffle of my hair then she added, 'Oh, Lyndsay said to give her a call about tonight. She's at her dad's.'

'I'll go put my trainers on,' Sam said, remembering my helpful hint from the morning, and dashing out.

'He's in love,' I explained.

Instinct told me Sam was wasting his time. If Lynz was at her dad's, not her mum's as she was meant to be, she was five miles away in Rotherham. I dialled, prepared for the worst. She answered straight away. 'Hi?'

'Hi, it's me.'

'Aw, Suzanne, thanks for phoning. Listen, I can't come tonight.'

I did my best to hide my surprise. 'Let me guess— you're washing your hair?' She loved her hair. It was long and fair and washed almost more times than Man United changed strips in a season.

'Ho! Ho! Actually, Jez is here and . . . '

I supressed a groan. This was about the millionth time she'd done this to me now. I never did this to her when I was going out with a bloke. She'd turned into Simper Girl since dating Jepson. 'I thought he'd gone to Leeds?' I said. That had been the whole deal behind tonight—a Saturday together without me playing gooseberry.

'Oh, don't ask! Anyway, he's here and Dad's going out, so . . . ' Her voice trailed off into a whisper.

'So you can "make out",' I furnished for her in my best American sitcom voice.

'Shh! Dad might hear.'

16

'I'll see you tomorrow, then?'

'Tomorrow?'

'Yes, tomorrow, the day we'd arranged to revise for our French orals,' I prompted.

'Er . . . I know but I've kind of promised Emm I'd go out with her—she's really down since Chink dumped her for that girl who sells the *Big Issue*. You can come with us, though—round Meadowhall.'

Emm was Lyndsay's dad's girlfriend's step-daughter. Relationships were complicated in the Fritton households. 'No,' said the girl who had no problems at all, 'I'll give it a miss; see you Monday.'

'We're setting off at eleven if you change your mind.'

'Sure.' I almost hung up, then faltered, 'Lynz, do you remember Karenna Sheldon from school?'

'Yeah; wasn't she always hanging out in the bogs with that weird . . . Jez, pack it in! I'm talking to Suzanne!' Lyndsay squealed.

Jez shouted 'hi' down the phone and went back to doing whatever he was doing to make her snort like a pig in truffle heaven. It was obvious there was no point continuing so I shouted 'see you' and hung up. I trundled upstairs to run my bath, telling myself that James Dean would make a better listener anyway.

I had just poured the last of my dewberry foam gel into the tub when Dad shouted me to the phone. 'If it's Lyndsay tell her I'll call later,' I yelled downstairs, 'I'm going to have a bath.'

'It's Karenna from work,' Dad shouted back up to me.

I froze, staring blankly at the top of his head. 'No!' I mouthed silently. 'No!'

Dad looked at me, mildly puzzled, before pressing the receiver to his ear again. 'Sorry, love, she must have gone out without me realizing. Do you want to leave a message? . . . All right, love, I'll tell her.' He hung up. 'Says it wasn't important—just something about work. Why wouldn't you talk to her?'

17

I frowned, stammering out the first excuse I could think of. 'She's a bit . . . backward,' I said, resorting to one of Grandma's words. 'Tina says she likes to phone new people she meets at the salon. If you talk to her once you never get rid of her . . . Tina said not to encourage her.'

'What's she doing in the salon in the first place?'

'Care in the Community . . . Tina's . . . into that sort of thing.'

Dad sloped off to worry about my steely attitude to the socially challenged. 'It wouldn't have hurt you to speak to the poor lass,' he mumbled.

My legs shook as I stared down into the hallway.

Everything had changed.

The hallway still needed decorating; my school bag was still under the telephone table where I'd chucked it yesterday, my family loved me, and Wednesday were still crap but everything had changed.

4

'*Match of the Day*'s on in five minutes,' Dad yawned from my bedroom doorway.

I glanced up from the scrapbook I was reading and shook my head. 'I'll give it a miss tonight, thanks.'

'Everything OK? You've been very quiet.'

I grinned reassuringly, 'I'm fine, just a bit tired.'

His face creased with concern. 'You don't have to work Saturdays, you know, if you find it too much, especially only weeks from your exams. I know you don't get as much allowance as some of your friends but . . . '

'Dad, don't worry, I'll be fine; I'm a genius, remember!'

'Yes, well . . . ' His eyes rested on the scrapbook. 'Are you still collecting those?' he asked in surprise.

'Yes.'

He scratched the side of his neck, frowning. 'Isn't it all a bit . . . depressing?'

I shrugged, focusing on the newspaper clipping. 'Boy of ten in suicide attempt' ran the headline. It was the most recent of dozens of stories I'd volunteered to collect for Mrs Parminter's Personal, Social and Religious Education lessons. 'They're just useful to have in discussions. Kids find it easier to open up if they know others have been through the same experience.' Said she.

Dad sighed. 'I know, and I think it's great that you do all this mentoring stuff for the school but I wish you'd, well, do something a little lighter as a hobby; swimming or ten pin bowling.'

19

'I watch United whenever I can afford it,' I argued.
'Now that's more a cry for help than a leisure activity!' he teased.
'Says the man who keeps maggots in the fridge!' I retorted. Dad and I had an understanding. He tolerated my love of the beautiful game, which he hated, so long as I didn't liberate his fishing bait, which I hated, into the back garden. I was left alone with a 'ha!' and returned to the cutting.

'Bullies changed my son from an easy-going sweet-natured child to a nervous wreck,' said Teresa Davies from Jack's hospital bedside yesterday. 'The school turned a blind-eye to what was going on. I was told what Jack was going through was nothing more than normal horseplay between friends. If it was just horseplay, why did my son try to hang himself with his dressing gown cord?'

I'll tell you why, Mrs Davies. Because the thought of never waking up, never having another birthday or Christmas, or even seeing you again was preferable to going to school every day and facing those so-called 'friends'.

I gazed sadly at the picture of her son, searching for 'the reason': the jam-jar-bottom specs or goofy teeth or pudgy fat cheeks or too-geeky clothes or too-trendy clothes or skin the 'wrong' colour—one clue as to why he was picked on in the first place. Nothing. Maybe, like me, he'd just been in the wrong place at the wrong time.

I closed my eyes and leaned against James Dean's legs, taking myself back to my first day at Steetley with Lynz, Patchouli Moxon, and Zoe Carpezza—all friends from juniors who had moved up with me. 'Gotta go!' I'd yelled and headed for the Toilet Block.

'You could wee for England, you could!' Patchouli called after me. They all knew about my weak bladder from primary school where I'd been the only pupil allowed to leave class for the loo without having to ask.

I dashed through the scratched, maroon door;

bursting. There was a yell and I realized I'd banged into someone but I daren't stop or I'd wet myself. I shouted 'sorry' and careered into the nearest cubicle. I had almost finished when the door was kicked open and Karenna stood there, staring; her cheeks red and angry. I blinked, thinking how pretty she was.

'You 'it me!' she snarled.

'Sorry—it was an accident,' I apologized.

Suddenly she stepped closer and flicked her finger savagely into my cheek. It made a popping sound. 'Sorry—it was an accident,' she mimicked. Behind her, two other girls snickered.

'Do it again, Karenna,' one of them said. She had a rotund, empty face. Fiona Featherstone, I later discovered.

'Yeah, Karenna, show the little snot what happens when you mess with us,' added the third. Jamillah.

Karenna leant towards me again, coming closer and closer as I tried to shrink back against the cistern. I could picture vividly, over five years on, the outline of her bra through her white blouse and the smell of cigarettes on her breath; feel the sting of her nail as she dug it into my neck. Hear myself whisper obediently as she demanded to know my name.

'Suzanne.'

'Suzanne what?'

'Fish.'

That had them rolling in the aisles. 'Well, guess what? Me and my mates'll be watching you from now on. Every time you take a pissy, Fishy!'

'Why?' I'd asked, more confused than anything at the time.

She had stood back and smiled fetchingly. 'No reason.'

I opened my eyes and gently rubbed my hand across Jack Davies's face. I bet Jack never knew the reason, either, but at least he followed the main rule—tell someone. Dur-brain here never told a soul. I'd just plummeted head-first into the role of victim, enduring everything jabbed into me by those three girls as if it was their divine right to do so. Perhaps if they hadn't caught me so early on I would have been a bit wiser, a bit more aware that it wasn't normal practice to be constantly stared at or pinned into a corner and have death threats hissed into your ear or phlegm coughed up into your school bag.

I should have been able to confide in Mum and Dad but things were all upside-down at home. Sam had been born four weeks before I started at Steetley. He wasn't planned, baby Sam, and I found out later Mum had even considered a termination because Dad had only just come off the dole, money was tight, and she was the main breadwinner as well as being forty-four. She didn't go through with it in the end but she had a difficult labour that left her ill and depressed for months after.

Dad did all the feeding and changing and getting up in the night, so he was exhausted. Chris thought the whole thing was disgusting and went into a major strop, especially after the cot was moved into his bedroom. I still had my bladder thing which meant occasionally I still wet the bed so, all in all, the atmosphere in the Fish household at the time was pretty tense.

And the longer the bullying went on, the harder it became to say anything, to have to explain why I hadn't spoken out earlier. Something hard and solid and stubborn inside prevented me from taking my shame into the house and exposing it—especially as I was winning so much praise, both at school and home, for my academic achievements. Somewhere along the line I had discovered the bruises didn't hurt so much if the brain was absorbed in extra helpings of quadratic equations and creating dazzling projects on saving the rainforest. It was also my way of proving to Sheldon I wasn't the thick cretin she repeatedly called me.

The resulting merit marks and outstanding reports and instructions to 'phone Grandma/Auntie Janet/ Uncle Ian and tell them how well you've done' wrapped me in a protective glow of approval which I didn't want to risk losing. In my warped sense of logic I worked out that if I did confess to the negative I'd lose the positive.

I should have told my friends. Lyndsay, especially, who never took any lip from anyone, might have helped, but her parents were pulling her apart during their divorce and she didn't know what day it was herself half the time. I did vaguely mention it on occasions, dropping hints casually into our conversation. 'What would you do if someone kept calling you names?' I'd ask. Her answers were invariably and inevitably unhelpful. 'Call them names back' or 'Just ignore it'. I felt like a feeble wimp for even asking. After that I began to snap at her for not being a mind-reader, walking off in a 'mardy' if she dared to tease me about one tiny thing. We often fell out, not speaking to each other for days until Patch or Zoe negotiated a peace deal.

By spring I'd started the skiving game, barely completing a full week again until Karenna suddenly left at the end of the following summer. Meanwhile, every day at school was filled with dread as I wondered what was waiting behind the scratched maroon doors.

I should have been able to tell a teacher at least? My form tutor, for instance. I wish! Mr Penny was pathetic; the sort of teacher who shouted threats but never carried them out. He'd allow the tough kids to steal his sandwiches and eat them in front of him while he'd pick on the quiet ones for not having their shirt tucked in. I still find it difficult to be civil to him if I pass him in the corridor.

I did ask once. I was trying to escape from Them after Jamillah had tried to slide her hand down my pants to see whether I had any pubic hair, her fingers lingering longer than even my compliant self was prepared to accept. Somehow I had struggled free, but with Karenna in hot pursuit I had crashed straight into Mr Penny, making him scald himself with his tea. 'Go steady, Suzanne!' he barked. Karenna was right behind.

'She's chasing me,' I bleated.

'Come here, Karenna,' he demanded irately, raising my hopes.

I watched as Karenna closed in on my form tutor. She was in Year Ten by then, well-developed and sexy. Mr Penny dipped his peppermint teabag endlessly in and out of his Dennis the Menace beaker, asking for an explanation.

'It was just a bit of fun, Mr Penny. I'm ever so sorry.' She smiled shyly at him, brushing her uplifted breasts against his elbow. He blushed. So did Dennis the Menace.

'Yes . . . well . . . just be careful . . . both of you. This tea's hot. Off you go.'

So off we went, for more fun.

I sighed heavily and closed the scrapbook.

'Want my advice, honey?' James Dean suddenly piped up.

'Not particularly.'

'Forget about it.'

'Forget about it?'

'Sure. Ain't no good looking back all the time. Look forward. You've got your whole life ahead of you. Why waste time on that bitch?'

'You haven't got a clue, have you?'

' 'bout what?'

'She's called home.'

'So?'

'I could cope when it was at school because I could

24

always come home, to my haven, but she's even invaded that this time.'

'Only if you let her.'

'Yeah, right.'

Like I had a choice.

5

Monday was supposed to be my best day at school but I still hadn't managed to shake off Karenna's invisible presence, no matter how much I tried. Although she hadn't phoned again, I felt haunted and had barely slept for the past two nights. Part of me had already decided I wouldn't be going back to Snippits but another part of me resented that decision. Star Mentors didn't cop out. I didn't know what to do.

I arrived outside Lab 2 at the same time as the chemistry teacher, Mr West. Mr West was American and one of my favourite tutors, famous for his foul ties and failure to understand why you shouldn't tell English kids to keep their 'fannies' still.

Today I was greeted with a 'Cheer up, Sue, it might never happen. Grab these,' before our folders were thrust into my hands. Mr West then proceeded to unlock the lab door, leaving the rest of us to follow. Once inside I released the folders where they spilt like lava across the front bench. 'Would you give those out for me?' he asked, already walking towards the blackboard, knowing I'd obey.

I began to dish out the tattered recordings of two years' coursework, secretly glad of the task because it meant I had an excuse to talk to Lee. If anything would cheer me up, it would be a smile from him.

Lee Anderson was gorgeous, sporty, clever, friendly, gorgeous, black, sensitive, gorgeous. Only two things stood in the way of my achieving eternal happiness with this demigod: 1) I knew he saw me as a sad boff—a condition to be pitied or mocked in a school like ours; 2) He was already going out with someone.

Eventually, I came to Lee's folder. Flashy lettering, declaring his love for Billy-Jo Pavlic, swamped the entire cover. Billy-Jo was a year below us but looked at least twenty-three. I couldn't even dislike her because she was a fellow mentor and always friendly towards me. Damn her. 'Hi,' I said trying to be as cool as possible as I slid Lee's folder to him.

He glanced up, killing me with his beautiful brown eyes. 'Hi. All right?'

'Yeah,' I responded, 'you?'

'Been better,' he shrugged, flicking open his folder with the back of his hand.

'The boy's been dumped,' Lee's mate, Kevin Cooper informed me, shaking his head in sheer disbelief.

I blushed instantly at this long-awaited news. 'Sorry,' I said quietly, my heart racing.

Kevin flung an arm of support around the dumped one's shoulders, 'He'll be all right, won't you, Anders? After a few nights with the boys, talent spotting. Out with the old, in with the new, like always?'

Lee threw his friend what can only be described as an extremely filthy look and stared up at me, puzzled. 'You're intelligent, Suzanne; explain to me why every other girl I've been out with slanders me for not being "committed" but the one girl I really, really care about finishes with me for being too intense?'

'I don't know,' I replied in total honesty, thinking Billy-Jo must be mental. Too intense? I'd have settled for 'remotely interested'.

'Too intense,' he repeated in disbelief. Kevin raised a pair of flummoxed eyebrows and I raised mine in return. As calmly as I could, I dealt out the remaining folders and sat down.

For once, I barely listened to Mr West's instructions as he fired out details on a test next Monday. Something

27

about chemical reactions, combustion, blah-blah-blah. I knew it all anyway.

The boff's brain was computing only one item of information and one item only: he was free! After months of being with Billy-Jo I was in with a chance. A bedroom window of opportunity. Lee'd wanted my opinion, not Kevin's, hadn't he? All he had to do from now on was ask and I'd be there in his hour of need, mopping his brow and any other bits that got hot and sweaty, listening and sympathizing. Then one day he'd look up at me and say 'Suzanne, Suzanne, what a complete nerd I've been all this time . . . '

It was the best chemistry lesson I'd ever had.

I was on mentor duty first break. Unfortunately, as I shared mentor duty with the all-male Mr Brunskill, my first task was checking the girl's Toilet Block. Reluctantly I pushed open the door and sniffed. Damp, disinfectant, and the lingering odour of decades of cigarette-smoking, menstruating girls clung to me like a bad dream. I hated this place, even though the lavatories had been renewed and the cubicle doors now locked, it was still the pits. I didn't plan to stay long. Reminders of Sheldon were not going to interrupt my dreamy state of mind this time.

Surprisingly, I was not the first to arrive. In the far corner, Patchouli Moxon was back-combing Zoe Carpezza's hair in front of the big mirror. I smiled, instantly grateful for their presence. We had stayed close friends until Year Ten, when they had discovered school hours clashed with pub opening times. Their attendance was the worst on record at Steetley, a fact of which they were both very proud. 'Are you pupils at this school?' I asked poshly, in a near-as-dammit imitation of Mrs Parminter.

'God, Fishy, don't do that!' Patchouli gasped, almost dropping the comb.

'I haven't seen you two for yonks!' I said, settling down on to the sanny bin next to them, drinking them in. Naturally, they were in uniform—trouble was it wasn't Steetley uniform. Today they were dressed entirely in black; combat trousers, jumper, leather studded jackets, stomping boots, topped by a semi-circle of studs and earrings edging their ears like chromium cornish pasties.

'Welfare Officer got you in court again?' I said, hazarding a random guess.

'Yep,' they chorused without further elaboration.

'Where's Lynz?' Zoe asked, changing tack.

'Art.'

They both sniggered. 'Art? She gets out of bed for art?' Mr Penny took art. Enough said. Patchouli continued to tug away at Zoe's hair. She had dyed it deep green which had the unfortunate effect of highlighting her pale, acne-prone skin. Not that it bothered her. Nothing seemed to faze either of them and I envied them for it.

Doors banged as one group of girls after another trooped in to escape the cold. They stared furtively at Patch and Zoe, impressed but nervous at what they saw. Indifferent to the attention, the aliens declared they were going for a smoke behind Hut Seven and invited me to join them. 'I will if I get a chance,' I said.

A group of Year Tens clustered round the mirror, pinning me into the corner. One of them leaned across my chest to hand her mate a tampon. It seemed a good time to leave but right on cue, Lyndsay bounded in. 'Hi! Thought I'd catch you in here,' she greeted, pushing her hair back from her face and smiling her pineapple lip-gloss smile. 'You should've come to Meadowhall yesterday. Emm got off with one of the waiters in the Denver Diner,' she gushed, rushing past me and heading into one of the loos.

'Yeah?' I replied casually. Who needed waiters?

'Yeah. He's dead fit. And the guy with him was quite tasty, too. You could have got fixed up.'

'I have my own plans, thank you,' I said mysteriously.

'Oh yeah? What sort of "plans"?'

29

I caught sight of the tampon-giver listening with interest. Maybe a friend of Billy-Jo's.

'I'll tell you later. I'll be behind the Craft Block,' I shouted.

There came the sound of flushing water and the door opened. 'All right, hold your horses, I'll come with you.' Lyndsay wasn't a mentor, thought it was all 'sad' but usually accompanied me anyway.

I shrugged and waited for her to wash her hands. I told her about Patch and Zoe. 'They look more far-out every time I see them,' I said admiringly.

It was Lyndsay's turn to shrug. 'I prefer clean to far-out,' she said, a bit snottily I thought.

We walked round to the Craft Block where there were no signs of smoking, sexual activity, or stabbings by either pupils or teachers. I was tempted to tell Lynz about Lee but hesitated, knowing from past experience she'd be on the case in a flash, negotiating terms in that subtle way of hers. Lunchtime—the dining room—the Fritton shout echoing its way between Lee at the sandwich bar and me at the hot meals counter. 'Suzanne says she'll meet you in Fitzalan Square at seven, Lee! OK? She's paying!' I shuddered and asked her why she'd been at her dad's instead of her mum's on Saturday.

'Oh, Mum started on about Dad never giving her enough maintenance and I told her that she had a cheek seeing as she'd just come back from Ibiza with Terry so she flew into one of her "why shouldn't I have a holiday abroad now and again?" deals . . . '

I tuned in and out of Lyndsay's rantings, half wishing I hadn't asked. Finally she ended with . . . 'So I phoned Dad and he came to fetch me.'

'Why didn't you come to our house, though? You could have slept over on the futon.'

'I know but . . . I just didn't feel like . . . '

'Like what?'

'Being with the Bisto family. I always feel I'm having

my nose rubbed in it when I stay with you—you're all always so happy.'

I would have accepted her excuse if her neck hadn't flushed the tell-tale fibber's flush I knew so well. 'Give over, Lynz. Your mum was staying in and your dad was going out so you knew you'd have his house free to be with Jezzy who'd cancelled going to Leeds for "whatever" reason,' I said scornfully.

'Well, there was that,' she admitted, picking strands of hair from her sweatshirt, 'but before you start I've got some good news. How do you fancy coming to Newcastle with Jez's basketball team a week on Sunday?'

'Why is that good news?'

'Because Lee Anderson is the captain and I'll make sure you get to sit next to him on the minibus. I don't think Billy-Jo's going—her name's not on the list.' And we all knew why. Lynz squeezed my arm and began steering me towards the main school before continuing, 'Anyway, you've got to go—I'm not watching sweaty men throw a ball at each other all afternoon on my own. We're going to find a Multiplex after and have a meal or I wouldn't bother. It shouldn't cost more than fifty quid altogether.'

'Fifty quid! Who's driving the minibus? Dennis Rodman?' I asked incredulously.

'What's the problem? You're on mega bucks now, Saturday girl.'

'Joke.'

'I can always lend you it, if you're short.'

Yeah, and I'd never hear the end of it. Trying to keep up with Lyndsay was why I'd needed a job in the first place. Lyndsay only had to snap her fingers at either home and hey presto! money appeared without any reference to it not growing on trees, unlike in the Fish residence. By earning extra cash I'd hoped to end her condescending offers to bail me out. I couldn't flounder so soon. 'No thanks, I'll manage,' I said.

31

'So you're coming?'

'Why not?'

'Great!'

I spent the rest of the day fantasizing about Lee, me, and the back seat of a darkened minibus. 'Nice to see someone's happy today,' Mrs Parminter grinned at me as I floated past her office on the way to English.

'Someone is,' I agreed.

6

All I had to do was find fifty quid. I already had twenty but that was meant to be for new clothes. Perhaps one of my kind, sweet parents would stump up the money in their daughter's bid to get a love-life.

Unfortunately, back at the ranch, I walked straight into an ambush. In the far corner stood Mum, armed with her pointy finger and glass of Croft's Original. The Croft's said, 'I have finished work and I am relaxing.' The pointy finger said, 'By relaxing I mean hassling the kids,' and was aimed at Chris, slouched defensively in the armchair.

'Suzanne, help me out here,' Mum announced, her eyes twinkly-but-meaningful. 'Am I right in thinking that to get an A-level it helps if you revise before, rather than after, the exam?'

'Why?' I asked warily.

'Why? Because your brother here seems to think you can. He seems to think that because he already had six points from last year's dismal effort he won't have to work that much to get the mere further sixteen points it transpires he needs this year to get into Nottingham.'

'I never said that,' Chris countered calmly, 'I said, "At least I've got a start".'

That really got the finger going. Mum's response was bruising. 'Christian, I know you. You are a lazy little swine who leaves everything to the last minute and then wonders why he isn't already at college like normal nineteen year olds.' Mum was desperate for us to act disgracefully in a student bed-sit somewhere. She always got swoony when she recounted her days as a trainee nurse in the Crimea. Inevitably, she launched into one of her 'a good education is vital now more than ever' routines for the next five minutes.

All of which made zero impression on the bro. He reached forward and brushed some dried mud off his boot. 'Yeah, yeah. I've heard it all before.'

'I mean it, Chris. You've got to buckle down, now, not in a few weeks' time. You've got to get a study plan worked out and all your notes up-to-date and you've got to spend more time at home like Suzanne does and . . . '

Oh no! Not the old playing off of one sibling against another bit. Fatal. I waited for the explosion. Chris gathered his folders from around his feet and stood up. His eyes, dark and angry now, drilled into Mum's. 'Next time you lecture me on "normal" nineteen year olds, just remember normal nineteen year olds don't share bedrooms with five-year-old junior sycophants, petal.'

Petal, as in those found on a Venus fly-trap, narrowed her eyes. 'Well, I'm sorry we don't all live in detached six-bedroomed Edwardian villas off the Eccleshall Road but that's life—as you'll soon learn.'

I thought Chris would burst a lung at this snide reference to Sarah's house but instead he withdrew a piece of paper from the top of his folders and handed it to Mum.

'What's this?' she asked.

'My study plan, sweetheart,' he replied in his 'Sam' voice.

Mum squinted at the tatty bit of paper in her hand. 'Oh,' she said shortly.

'Where is Sam?' I asked, worried in case he heard.

'After School Club,' Mum mumbled.

'And here's the history assignment I was meant to hand in today,' Chris continued, waiting coolly until she received the baton of sheets. I could make out multi-coloured felt-tipped lines and a drawing of a huge head with curly hair adorning the title page with the word

'Sma' next to it. Mum gnawed her bottom lip. 'Oh dear.' Chris just stood there, festering like a ripe boil.

The slightest hint of tension at home made me jittery, reminding me of those awful days just after Sam had been born. I waited uneasily, wondering what I could do to stop the argument, to make things better. 'I'll share with Sam until Chris's exams are over. I don't mind moving out, honest,' I interrupted.

Chris rewarded me with a murderous scowl. 'Oh, thank you so much, Suzanne. Naturally my precious, gifted sister will donate her room full of posters of dead clichés and second-rate soccer teams to the family degenerate,' he scoffed.

'I'll take them with me,' I said instantly.

'Damn right you will, honey,' James Dean added.

'It's not a bad idea, Christian,' Mum said.

Big bro disagreed. 'It is, actually—it's a pathetic idea from the Queen of the Martyrs. And don't call me Christian! It sucks! You might as well've called me Jesus!' he bellowed.

With that statement, he rushed past me and thudded upstairs. Mum stared, glassy-eyed, at the pages in her hand as Dad peered cautiously round the door. 'Everything all right?' he asked, instantly frowning at the sight of his wife re-filling her glass.

'Oh, fine,' Mum replied sarcastically, 'your eldest son has a name that "sucks" and your youngest son is apparently a sycophant on top of which I had my credit card rejected in front of dozens of people in Morrison's this afternoon but apart from that life couldn't be better.'

I sighed heavily as what remained of my good mood disappeared faster than the Croft's. News of rejected credit cards was not what I wanted to hear.

'You'll go steady with that, won't you?' Dad said, nodding at the bottle behind Mum. He was funny about alcohol; he didn't drink at all. I think it had something to do with his dad, Grandad Leonard, who pegged it

35

when I was little, but it's on the best-not-mentioned list along with Margaret Thatcher and my bed-wetting days. Mum grew angrier and started on about gas bills while Dad listened wearily with the occasional bark to show he wasn't a totally passive wally.

I retreated upstairs to do what I did best: recede into my world of schoolwork and converse with James D. 'I know what you mean, honey,' JD sighed, smouldering with concern for me, 'things weren't too hot when I was a kid. Ma died when I was eight . . . '

'That must have been awful.'

'Then the episode with Pier Angeli later on . . . '

'Yeah, I know—the only woman you ever loved . . . '

'Talking to yourself's the first sign of madness,' Chris announced from my doorway.

'What's the second? Not minding your own business?' I snapped back, feeling embarrassed.

He gazed steadily at me, 'No, giving things away you still want—like bedrooms.'

'I was only trying to help,' I replied.

He scratched the back of his neck. 'I know . . . I came across a bit harsh but why do you always have to be the one who—'

'Who what?'

Unfortunately, whatever I always 'had to' was interrupted by the heart-thudding sound of the phone ringing. Like Pavlov's dog, I reacted to that sound in only one way now—sheer panic. 'You get it,' I croaked.

Chris had already ambled out, presuming it was Sarah. My breathing deepened as I waited, willing the call to be for him. 'Yo, bint! It's for you,' he shouted up to me.

'Who is it?' I asked from the top of the stairs.

'Don't know, don't care,' he replied miserably.

'Well, was it male or female?' I probed, passing him halfway.

'Well, it's not gonna be male is it, if they're asking for you?'

'Drop dead, Jesus.'

'Say please.'

Tentatively, I lifted the receiver, 'Hello?' I whispered. There was a clicking followed by a rasping sound, then nothing. My heart pounded. 'Hello?' I repeated, ready to hang up.

'Hello? Fishy?'

My legs almost buckled with relief—it was Patchouli. 'Hi! What's up?'

'What's up? My dad's mobile phone is crapola for a start—I can hardly hear you. Can you hear me?'

'Just.'

'Listen, Zoe and me are going to Benders on Saturday to celebrate doing a full week at school. Do you and Lynz fancy coming?'

I glanced towards the kitchen door to make sure it was closed. Benders was a night club in the city centre with a reputation for trouble. There was no way I'd be allowed to go anywhere near. 'Lynz is seeing Jez on Saturday,' I began.

'Just you, then. Even better.'

The idea of spending a Saturday night out with them filled me with both excitement and terror. Quickly, I tried to think of another excuse that would allow me to be with them until they departed for Benders that didn't sound as feeble as 'my dad won't let me'. 'I . . . I'm working at Snippits on the Piazza until half-five . . . maybe we could meet early on?' I suggested.

'Great, see you then, then. Wear what you dare!'

'Patch . . . I—'

But she'd gone, mobile and all.

So, princess, you are working at Snippits until half-five, are you?

It looked as if I had a date with destiny after all.

7

All too soon it was Saturday morning again. Mum woke me up this time, shaking her head as she swapped my three empty cups for one full mug of steaming coffee. 'I wondered where all these were,' she tutted, clanking the empties together before perching on the edge of my bed.

'What time is it?' I mumbled.

'Twenty to seven. My lift's late again.'

There was a pause. I opened one eye, squinted at her, then burrowed further down in bed, not wanting to get up. She stroked my face, something she hadn't done in a long time. 'You're all growing up so fast,' she moaned. 'Here you are, getting up for your Saturday job. Another year and you'll be out every night, going to clubs, wanting to sleep over with your boyfriends.'

'I'm not waiting a year!' I retorted.

She sighed. 'I delivered a baby for a fourteen-year-old girl yesterday. Fourteen, Suzanne. She still had braces on her teeth.' Young mothers always saddened Mum—she felt they were throwing their lives away.

Outside, a car horn blared, and she stood up, smoothing down her starched uniform. 'Oh, well, I'd better be off. Remind your dad to take the meat out of the freezer. Don't forget I'm going for a staff meal straight after work so I won't see you until late. Take care.'

'I'll be late, too, remember. I'm meeting friends for a coffee after work.'

'Enjoy yourself.'

I intended to but I had to survive a day with Karenna first.

The first thing I did when I arrived outside Snippits was check the front. Fortunately, all brickwork was clear. At least I didn't have that indignity to face. Tina had already opened up and Candy was mid towel-sniffing when I entered.

I glanced round but couldn't see Karenna. Tina and Candy both smiled at me and I felt comforted by their friendliness. 'Hello, Suzanne. Are you all right?' Tina asked.

'Yes, thanks.'

'Good.' She stared admiringly at me. 'I'd forgotten how lovely and tall you were. You ought to go in for modelling.'

I groaned inwardly. Why did people assume that because of my height, five-ten, I would automatically want to become a flipping model? There was nothing I'd less rather do. 'My brother thinks I look like an ironing board,' I said.

'Oh, brothers—what do they know? Take no notice.' She paused, frowning at the sinks behind me. 'Can you give those a quick wipe down before we get busy, Suzanne, then tidy up the Carmel range in the window—it looks like someone's been playing skittles with it.'

'OK.'

My boss then disappeared into the back room. Candy presented me with a bottle of Jif and a sponge. 'Karenna should've done them last night but she dashed off early,' she said in a low voice. 'You watch—Tina won't say a thing to her. I'd get it in the neck if I'd left them mucky.'

I rubbed away, model-like. 'Mmm,' I mumbled. I didn't want to be involved.

'I'm thinking of going freelance when Soroya's older. Going round old people's homes like Tina does on a Wednesday. Mind you, I don't know if I'd have the patience . . . '

'Mmm,' I repeated.

'I don't know enough about hip replacements,' she nattered.

'No.'

'You're very quiet today,' Candy remarked, pulling loose hair from brushes and combs.

'Mmm,' I said.

Karenna arrived, swanning in like a film star. I glanced up at her quickly, then concentrated hard on the limescale around one of the taps. She said a brief 'hi' to us then headed for the staffroom. 'She's been weird all week,' Candy informed me, jerking her head in Sheldon's direction. 'Nearly jumps out of her skin every time the door opens.'

'I know the feeling,' I muttered.

'I think it's her dad, Bernie—he's just come out on parole, y'know,' she hissed in my ear.

'Oh,' I said shortly, wishing Candy would belt up or at least get on to some neutral topic like chemical castration. The less I knew about Her the better. Apart from one or two bad dreams, total paranoia when the phone rang, and reliving the past, I'd managed fairly well all week. If I was absolutely honest, only one thing had kept me from walking straight past Snippits this morning—the thought of the wage packet I'd get at the end of the day for the Newcastle trip.

'You'll rub the enamel off, Suzanne!' Tina exclaimed, bringing me back to the present with a jolt. 'You were miles away.'

'Sorry.'

'By the way, your football scarf's still in the staffroom from last week.'

'Oh—of course.'

'Karenna phoned to let you know but you weren't in.'

40

'Erm . . . no, I wasn't.'

I swallowed hard as the reason for the phone call was explained. So that was it—she hadn't been stalking me at all as my fertile imagination had led me to believe— just calling to tell me I'd left my scarf. Mystery solved. Deal with that, Suzanne.

Karenna entered then, thrusting her trolley full of curlers and solutions by my side. I tensed, immediately guarded and alert, despite the revelation.

'My tongs are missing and I've got Jackie Paine at ten to. Where are my tongs?' she demanded of no one in particular.

'They can't be far,' Tina reasoned. 'Help her look for them, Suzanne.'

I stirred a few curlers warily around on the bottom tray of the trolley, careful to avoid eye contact with her as she hunted for the tongs. She seemed flustered, her hyper-active hands flicking in every direction until she inevitably knocked a box of hairpins on to the floor, scattering them with a 'sush' across the vinyl. 'Shit . . . pick them up for me,' she ordered bluntly, then walked off.

I gazed at the floor, seeing not hairpins but sandwiches. I was that skinny kid again, back in the corner bog, having stupidly risked the chance They might not be in there. I just never seemed to learn.

Fiona Featherstone had emptied my lunch box behind the U-bend of the lavatory, where they lay clumped among the debris. 'Pick them up for me,' Karenna barked. Of course, I obeyed; the one thing I had learned was to follow instructions immediately—life was easier that way.

Reaching my arm around the dark, greasy pipe, I levered my tomato sandwiches out one at a time, my nose wrinkling at the grit and hair adhered to them. 'Might as well eat 'em before they go off,' Featherstone grunted.

Karenna smirked. 'No—I've got a better idea. Give her your ham sarnie, Fev. Make her eat that instead.'

'What for?' Fiona had grumbled. She liked her food. 'I've heard she's a vegetarian. This'll prove whether she is or not.'

I ate the ham. I can still taste it, slimy-skin, pig meat. Karenna just laughed, but her eyes were filled with disgust. 'You really are pathetic,' she said.

Tell me something I didn't know.

Slowly, I began to pick up the pins.

I spent as long on the window display as I dared, arranging then rearranging the plastic tubes and bottles into neat groups, pushing away my miserable past with each careful pairing of dry-scalp conditioners and split-end treatments. The task had a therapeutic effect, helping me to calm down, allowing me time to remind myself that I was sixteen, I had rights, I was not a victim any more and I didn't have to take anything from anybody. 'Just quit,' James Dean interrupted from out of nowhere but I couldn't quit because I'd been told to pick up some hairpins. Even Dad's union wouldn't support me on that one.

It seemed I had to decide whether to stay and take orders from a person I deeply detested and who, I finally admitted to myself, still scared me—or leave. If I was going to have flashbacks every time someone dropped hairpins, or think I was being stalked when all I'd done was leave a scarf behind, there was little point staying—I'd probably be sacked for incompetence anyway. I glanced through to the outside world between my award-winning display and the coat rack, telling myself I was only ever a plate-glass window away from freedom. I could go whenever I wanted.

Behind me, Tina, Candy, and Karenna were all busy with their clients, gabbling away about everything and nothing at all. Despite its dated appearance the salon was warm and cheerful. I knew Candy thought I was all right, and Tina was always pleasant and even Sheldon hadn't said or done anything either way, really. Not really. What could happen? Nothing. I'd stay—for now.

'Suzanne, coffee for Mrs Venn, please,' Tina called. Coffee for Mrs Venn. No problem.

The problems started after lunch with one of Karenna's clients called Nicky Pattinson. She had stood out as soon as she arrived, firstly because of her designer lime day-glo puffa jacket and second because of her booming, broad Yorkshire accent. 'Hiya, everybody!' she greeted effusively. 'In't it a grand day?'

I took her jacket and she gave me a confident, red-lipped grin. 'Are you new?'

I nodded, trying to match her smile.

'Thought so. If this lot give you any 'assle just point 'em in my direction. I'll "thrup" 'em for you.'

'Thanks,' I said, liking her at once.

Nicky's hair was long, like Lyndsay's, but a deeper chestnut colour which fanned out dramatically against the black protective cape Karenna fitted round her. Usually we Saturday assistants did that job but the junior stylist seemed to be taking this one all the way herself.

'Your hair's looking great,' Karenna enthused.

'I'm sick on it,' Ms Pattinson stated, flicking her head from side to side.

'What about a re-style?' Karenna suggested, combing through the long strands. 'There's a fantastic new shape I've been dying to try out. You'd be perfect for it. I'll show you the magazine.'

'Now don't start, Karenna. You know I will never have my hair cut short. I just want highlights to make me look even more beautiful than I am now, as if that's possible!' she boomed, daring anyone to disagree.

'Get the sample books,' Karenna said to me, disappointedly.

I didn't know what she meant. 'Where are they?'

'Under the desk.'

I couldn't find anything that looked like a book. Reluctantly, I told Karenna so. She scowled and came across, crouching beside me and frowning. 'There,' she hissed, pointing to two white folders on the top shelf, 'those are the sample books, idiot.' Swiftly, she reached across, banging her elbow into my arm as she grabbed for the samples. There was no apology, expected or given.

'Titian' was finally chosen as the new colour which was to make her client look even more beautiful. 'If I don't get a toy boy after this I shall want to know why,' Nicky informed everybody.

'I'll need B9,' Karenna said.

I looked at her dumbly.

'B9, the base tint. In the staffroom.'

'I don't know what to look for,' I said.

The junior stylist gave a light, false laugh. 'Honestly!' she said, resting a hand gently on Nicky's shoulder. 'If you want anything doing . . . ' Curling her index finger in my direction, she beckoned me to follow her.

Once in the staffroom she closed the door behind us, turned on the light switch, and pointed to a shelf high above the sink which I had overlooked before. It was stacked with small white boxes. 'There,' she said in a low, familiarly dangerous voice.

'I didn't know. I've only been here two weeks, remember,' I said defensively. She stretched out her hand and reached deftly for one of the boxes. From it, she retrieved a small plastic bottle with B9 stamped on the lid.

As I turned to go back into the salon she grabbed my arm and fixed me with her violent blue eyes. 'Listen,' she said, 'that woman out there runs her own company—she's rolling in it—and she comes to my salon to have her hair done by me. She doesn't go to any of the flash places in town, she comes to me—me! So what I don't want is you messing everything up with your "it's-not-my-fault-I'm-new" crap. Understand?'

I didn't, but I nodded all the same. She released her grip. 'And stop looking at me like that, Suzanne Fish. You're not twelve any more!' With that, she switched off the light and flounced back to her client.

Even an hour later, when Nicky generously pressed a five pound tip into my hand, all I could feel was Karenna's touch, like sunburn, on my arm.

It was happening again and I felt as hopeless and stupid as ever. Forget Oprah, Mrs Parminter, Star Mentors, and PSRE. When you were scared, you were scared, and no amount of reading and role play and newspaper cuttings could take away that sick, twisted feeling you got in the pit of your stomach, no matter how old you were.

By five o'clock I had decided never to darken Snippits' doors again. I'd phone Tina mid-week and hand in my notice. I shrugged away the imagined feel of Lee's lips on mine in some Newcastle cinema and smiled apologetically as I received my second and final wages. 'Thanks,' I said to Tina.

'You've earned it,' she replied. 'You learn fast and you're polite. What's more, I trust you—last girl we had was more interested in the till than hairdressing, if you catch my meaning.'

I nodded. I didn't give a toss. I just wanted to go home.

As if sensing something was wrong, Tina glanced over her shoulder to where Karenna was throwing damp towels over the hairdryers. 'I know Karenna's been a bit snappy with you today but don't take it to heart, it's nothing personal—she's been the same with everyone. Poor lass is going through a rough time with her dad at the moment. Just bear with us, eh?'

'Sure,' I lied, glancing through the window, three feet from freedom.

'Anyway,' she said, returning to her normal tone, 'five pound tips aren't bad, are they?'

'Blooming not,' the ever-eavesdropping Candy observed, 'I wish that Nicky was one of my clients.'

'Wish away,' Karenna quipped acidly.

There was a sudden pounding on the window, making us all jump. Karenna immediately darted into the staffroom, banging the door loudly after her. 'Get rid of him, Tina, get rid of him!' she called plaintively through the thin plywood. Tina glanced at the window where Patchouli and Zoe's distorted faces were pressed horribly against the glass.

'Friends of yours?' she asked me coldly.

'Yes—sorry.'

She sighed. 'Off you go. See you next Saturday.'

I tried to keep a straight face as she walked towards the staffroom.

Candy nudged me playfully in the ribs, united by our common dislike of Karenna. 'Get them to do that again next week. I'll pay you!'

We were being cruel, I know, but it just felt so good seeing Sheldon scared stiff for once. As far as I was concerned, Sheldon's dad—or whoever 'he' was— deserved a medal. I said goodnight to Candy and headed out to meet my friends.

8

'What do you look like!' I gasped, creased up at the sight of them. In my honour, they had set their hair in multi-coloured bendy curlers.

'Don't you think it'll catch on, then?' Zoe asked, patting her rubbery locks with mock tenderness.

'Er . . . no,' I replied, turning to Miss Moxon, resplendent in a tight-fitting burgundy dress which made her boobs stand out like vacuum-packed beetroot. For my part, I was less radically attired, knowing I wasn't going to Benders later, though they didn't know this small detail yet. 'Do you two always go out this early? What is there to do at this time? Coffee?' I asked hopefully.

They pulled a face. 'Coffee? Girl, you obviously are unaware of the concept known as "Happy Hour". Happy Hour begins at five and ends at seven.'

'That's two hours,' I couldn't help pointing out.

'She's got a brain on her!' Zoe laughed, steering me in the direction of The Bricklayers Arms.

'Are we going in here?' I asked worriedly as she pushed open the dark oak door leading into the lounge.

'Well, Fishy,' Patchouli said evenly, 'we've tried having Happy Hour in a bus-stop but it just lacked something, somehow. Besides which, Zoe's Uncle Gilly works behind the bar here, and we feel it only fair to support him in his workplace by free-loading for all we can get.'

I took a deep breath, wondering whether this would be a good time to tell them I had never been in a pub

47

before, but thought better of it. I knew they saw me as a bit of a sad case anyway, what with being a boff and all that. 'What if someone asks for ID?' I questioned.

Zoe snorted. 'Like who, Suzanne? Look around.'

I did. We were in a large, square room with dark panelled walls and a hideous floral carpet. Vinyl padded seats lined the walls, broken at intervals by various doors leading to other rooms. At the far end, an empty bar, padded like the seats, awaited our custom. Apart from us and Zoe's uncle, the place was deserted. Good Taste 0, Atmosphere 0. Immediately I relaxed and asked for lends of make-up.

'What do you want to drink?' Patchouli asked as I headed for the Ladies.

'Erm . . . whatever you're having,' I said.

There was a pay phone between the Ladies and Gents loos, so I quickly called home. I wasn't going to turn into a teen rebel that fast.

Sam answered. 'Hello, House of a Thousand Pleasures,' he announced politely. Chris passing on his social skills again.

'It's Suzanne, Sam. Are you OK?'

'Yes. Are you home soon? I've made you a biscuit with midget gems on. I gived you all the orange ones.'

'Aww—thanks, mate. Listen, where's Dad?'

'Ironing my pyjamas.'

'Will you tell him I'll be home about nine o'clock not seven?'

I figured they'd want to be heading for town by then and meanwhile I'd have thought of a wimp-out clause.

'Can I come?'

'Not this time. Don't let anyone eat my biscuit, will you?'

'No.' His voice trailed away just as my money ran out. I hung up, shaking off the mild feeling of guilt.

Back in the lounge, Patchouli was handing round long glasses of a milky yellow liquid. 'Who else is coming?' I asked, counting six drinks.

'Nobody. It's Happy Hour, remember—two for the price of one. Cheers, cocker!' She nudged two of the glasses towards me and turned to the barman. 'Cheers, Gilly,' she called. The barman winked. He had long grey hair fastened back in a ponytail and a T-shirt announcing 'Footballers do it in their shorts'. His bare arms were muscular and well-defined. I thought of my dad, standing in front of the telly in his M&S jeans and shirt, ironing.

'Does he work out?' I asked.

Zoe smirked proudly and leaned forward to whisper. 'He did a lot of body-building in Armley. He's just come out for beating up a couple of "nowters" last year. They tried to sell him some smack—he won't have anything to do with drugs since his best mate OD'd at his house.'

'Oh,' I replied sagely, as if I had a clue. I'd been offered stuff at parties, of course, but when you've got a mother like mine, who gives you all the details of how a stomach is pumped, plus diagrams, you think twice before sucking a Strepsil.

Timidly, I reached for a glass and sipped. It tasted lovely, like creamy lemon sodas. 'This is nice, what is it?' I asked, thinking even Dad couldn't disapprove of these.

'It's called a Knock-out. It's Unc's speciality,' Zoe informed me.

I took another sip. 'This is really nice—much better than lager.' I had pinched half a can of Jez's lager at the New Year party but it had been too cold and sharp to enjoy. This 'Knock-out' was totally different.

'The beer drinking starts at seven, when prices revert to rip-off and Gil-boy's shift ends,' Patchouli said sadly.

'Till seven!' I said, lifting my glass in a toast. I felt happy and light-hearted. It was just so great to be with two friends after cowering near Karenna all day. The three of us clinked and Zoe began chatting on about school.

'How do you do it, Fishy? Day after day? It's just so boring!' She seemed genuinely interested.

'It's a means to an end, isn't it?' I began uncertainly. 'You need GCSEs to get a good job . . . '

'So why are there so many graduates working in burger bars?' Patchouli pounced. 'I'm telling you, Sue, the whole education-for-advancement argument doesn't work any more. Any thicko can get a degree now that every building with tall windows and a blackboard calls itself a university.'

Her argument niggled me because it made sense. I defended myself with wit. 'You've been saving that speech for ages—I can tell,' I retorted merrily, draining my glass. I hadn't realized I was so thirsty. 'By the way, girls, I don't want to talk about school. I know you both think I'm a sad boff, but—'

'We don't, Fishy,' Patchouli interrupted animatedly. 'We admire you. You work hard, even in that dung-heap. It's us that's taken the easy way out, we admit it. All I'm saying is we'll all be on the dole together, only you'll do joined up writing when you sign on.'

'You've got lovely handwriting!' I protested.

'Don't tell anyone,' she said, then pulled a sour face as a bunch of United supporters rattled in, talking loudly and smelling of fried onions and cold air. 'Oh, no, not this lot,' she moaned.

Zoe swivelled round. 'No, it was the away fans who trashed the place last week. These lot are the home team.'

'They're all morons dressed in nylon, whoever they support,' Patch stated flatly.

I turned round and grinned. I was feeling warm and very content with the world, and here were my fellow men, fresh from Bramall Lane. 'Who won?' I asked enthusiastically.

A few heads turned, registered Zoe and Patch's curlers, then continued to the bar but one guy, with a sharp haircut and a sweet face, grinned. 'Robbed them one–nil!'

'Yes! Who scored?'

'Fishy!' Patchouli tugged my arm in horror.

'What?'

'No football talk.'

'Why?'

'Because it's so-oo boring! Come to the pool room, this sec!'

Reluctantly I grabbed the last of my Knock-out and, smiling apologetically at the sharp-haired guy, followed my friends into a smaller room behind the lounge. 'I miss going to matches now I'm at Snippits,' I complained.

'Hey, yeah—what's it like? I always thought it was a bit of a Sweaty Betty's,' Patchouli stated, tugging her bendy curlers out and stuffing them carelessly into her shoulder bag.

I shrugged, feigning indifference. 'Well, you know, OK I suppose. Anyway, I'm jacking it in.'

'Aw, what for?'

I had finished my second Knock-out by now and stared sadly at the milky glass. They were so nice, those drinks, so refreshing. 'I can't remember,' I said, and laughed out loud.

Patchouli and Zoe exchanged glances. They still had nearly all their second Knock-outs left, I noticed. 'You two are slow drinkers, to say you're the experts,' I said, before adding that I thought their clothes were great.

'I'd better get the next round in then, seeing as Fishy's living up to her name,' Zoe announced.

'I'm known as "princess" in high quarters,' I informed her, giggling.

There was a look of concern on Patchouli's face. 'You do know Knock-outs have got whisky and wine in them, don't you?' she asked. 'Only I remember your dad was funny about alcohol.'

'Have they? Is he?' I said in surprise. 'Oh well.' I sighed happily. 'I wish I had boobs like yours,' I said, 'they're proper knockers—Knock-outs—aren't they?

51

Not like my fried eggs.' I prodded my chest with a beer mat.

Patch shook her head and laughed. 'Fancy a game of pool?'

'Why not? What do you do?'

Expertly, she set up the balls inside a plastic triangle then showed me how to chalk and hold the cue. Zoe returned with another half-dozen cocktails and some peanuts. 'Face-ache Frank's helping Uncle Gilly out at the bar so make sure you don't get him when it's your turn,' she advised. 'He'll charge you full price.'

'OK,' I said, and potted my first ever pool ball. 'It went in! It went in!' I yelled gleefully.

'You're supposed to sink the black one last, Fishy,' Patchouli informed me, casually potting every yellow bar one.

'This is great,' I said. 'I'm really, really having a good time.' Picking up my glass, I downed it in one.

'Go steady, Suzie. You've got to pace yourself. We've got all night.'

I shook my head—best to confess now, I reckoned. 'No-oo, I have told Sam I'm coming home by nine. He's made me a bidget mem biscuit. I love him loads, you know, and I love Lee Anderson but not in the wame say.'

We cracked up again. I couldn't believe how wonderful I felt. Alive and full of energy. Soon it was my turn to go to the bar. Confidently, I stood up, though wobbling slightly. Unc was already serving and I got Frank.

'Mmm?' he grunted.

I smiled radiantly at him. 'This is my first time at your lovely padded bra,' I confided, ignoring his sudden frown. 'And I would like two for the price of one happy hour Knock-outs, please.'

He twisted round and muttered something in Gilly's ear. Gilly shrugged and muttered back. Frank, wisely, didn't argue. Sullenly, he began mixing the cocktails and I watched, mesmerized, as he poured and measured, enjoying the whole experience until he asked for the money. I stared at him, stupified. 'That's half my wages!' I protested, handing over the cash reluctantly.

'Stick to lemonade in future, then,' he advised.

'I'll never get to Newcastle at this rate,' I grumbled.

I felt slightly dizzy. 'I'm going to make a phone call,' I announced, sliding the tray on to the table and picking up one of my drinks. 'Back in just a mo.'

'We'll be on the pool table,' Zoe informed me.

I strained to check the time on my watch. Quarter to seven. Lee might be home. Without thinking, I dialled his number. 'It's me, Suzanne Briony Fish,' I slurred.

'Oh, hiya, Suzanne. Are you all right?' He managed to hide his surprise at Brain Woman calling him quite well.

'I'm great,' I giggled, 'I'm in a pub.'

He laughed. 'I thought you sounded a bit high. Who are you with?'

'Zoe and Patchouli.'

'Oh. That crowd—don't go dropping any E's, will you?'

'Na' then, Lee, tha' knows we only drop us aitches in Yorkshire!'

He laughed loudly, filling me with confidence. 'Lee, will you sit with me on the minibus to Newcastle?'

There was a slight pause, just long enough in which to think twice. 'Sure,' he replied.

Sure! He said sure!

'I love you, Lee—have done for months,' I gushed.

'Are you serious?' he asked.

'Yes,' I said, then hung up.

I returned to the pool room, leaning against the pool table as Zoe was about to take a shot. 'Do you know who I'm working with?' I demanded.

'No.'

'Karenna Sheldon, that's who.' I frowned, puzzled as to where that bombshell had come from in relation to

53

the other bombshell I'd just dropped. My mind seemed to be flitting from one thing to another like a wasp trapped in a jar.

'Karenna Sheldon? That cow!' Zoe said, expertly potting the last red.

'Exactly. That cow!' I replied, chuffed she shared my opinion. I moved across to a corner seat. 'My dad could re-cover these for a very reasonable price,' I added, running my hands down the worn Dralon.

Patchouli shook her head and sat with me as Zoe nominated a pocket. 'She flicked me in the face once. I've never seen my dad so mad. He didn't half give it some when he went to school. She never did it again,' she said proudly.

'I remember when—' Zoe began, but I interrupted her rudely.

'What, you mean she only flicked you once?' I asked, staring at Patchouli in wide-eyed indignation. 'Once?'

'Of course. Nobody does that to me twice!'

'She did it to me loads! Loads!' I said, my voice rising and rising.

'But why? Why did you let her?'

'I didn't want to die,' I said, marvelling at their stupidity.

'What do you mean?' Zoe asked quietly, coming to sit next to me. She glanced questioningly at Patch, who shrugged lightly, as if to say she didn't have a clue, either.

Then, for the first time ever, I revealed all the things Karenna had done to me for those two years, right down to the ham sandwich incident. By the end we were all close to tears. 'Why didn't you tell us? How could you go through all that alone?' Patchouli asked in astonishment.

Zoe gazed at me. 'I feel depressed now,' she said.

I beamed broadly, wiping my eyes with the back of my wrist. 'Why? It doesn't matter, does it, cos I'm sitting with Lee on the minibus.'

'And then to end up in the same place!' Patch continued.

I waved my hand at her airily. 'I'm not going back. I won't have to see her again.'

My drinking buddy stood up, her eyes glinting. 'Oh, yes you are, Suzanne Fish! You have to. You have to go back or you'll never get rid of her. You have to tell her what she did to you. Otherwise your whole life is a . . . farce. All this Star Mentor business and workaholic stuff—it's all copping out. You have to go back!'

'You're right!' I shouted triumphantly, standing up with her. 'Let's go do it now!' I reeled slightly, holding on to the edge of the table to steady myself. 'But first, can someone stop the room from spinning?'

9

'It's gone dead dark!' I ranted when we tumbled out of The Bricklayers Arms. 'It was only a bit dark before but now it's dead dark.'

'That's because it's now night-time, Suzanne,' Zoe said slowly as if talking to a child. 'It gets dark at night-time.'

I slapped my forehead as if just remembering this very crucial fact. 'You're right. What time during night-time is it?' I asked.

'Time to get you home, sweetheart,' Patchouli said, letting rip with an ear-splitting whistle. Across the road, a taxi squealed to a halt.

'Sam calls me sweetheart, you know,' I informed them in a soppy voice as they each grabbed one of my arms and frog-marched me across to the cab.

'I can walk!' I protested, trying to ignore the dizzy whirling in my head.

We piled noisily into the back of the car. It smelt of wet dogs. A plastic skeleton danced jerkily from the driver's mirror. 'Where to, girls?' he asked.

'Hill Fort Avenue first, please,' Patchouli said.

'What about Benders?' I wanted to know.

Zoe hugged me close. 'Another time, Suze. You're going to bed.'

'Bed!' I sat up, indignant at such a suggestion. 'This cannot be!'

' 'ad a skinful, 'as she?' the driver asked.

'You keep your eye on the road, mister!' I growled at him, then giggled.

56

I began to feel very warm. I tried to focus on the skeleton but it wouldn't keep still at all. As we began the slow ascent up Roman Hill, I knew I'd have to puke any second. 'Let me out at the top,' I begged.

'You sure?' Patch asked worriedly. 'It's better if we take you all the way.'

'S'not far. S'no distance,' I managed to mumble.

The taxi drew up at the bottom of Hill Fort Avenue and I unceremoniously clambered out across Zoe's knees.

'I'll call you tomorrow,' Patchouli shouted as the car reversed.

'Have a nice day!' I called after her. Then I threw up. Then I threw up again. It was yellow and vile and runny and made my shoes wet but I felt brilliant now.

The heat and stuffiness of the taxi was blown away by the cold air. I made my way home, gulping in mouthfuls of the invisible nectar, practising bunny jumps on and off the kerb. I still felt giddy and 'high' as Lee had said. Knock-outs were epic—I was going to drink one every day for the rest of my life.

At last, I arrived home. And there was Old Bluey, Dad's converted ambulance, gleaming in the moonlight.

'Hello, Old Bluey!' I greeted.

Then, for some unknown reason, I decided it would be an excellent idea to sit on top of the clapped out thing. How I got up there, I'll never know. Somehow, I managed to haul myself on to the bonnet, scramble across the windscreen then slide on to the roof like a commando.

Slowly, carefully, I stood up. The view was breathtaking. I could see for miles, the power of electricity transforming the industrial valley below into a work of moving art as orange motorways snaked between streetlights and houselights, painting magical illuminated shapes.

'Good evening, Sheffield!' I cried out.

In my hand, an imaginary microphone sprang to life,

moving in an invisible arc through the stillness. At once, millions of voices responded, chanting back to me, their idol.

'I can't hear you!' I goaded. 'I said "Good evening, Sheffield!"'

The noise from the crowd was deafening. I decided to test them, push the boundaries of mega-stardom.

'Let's hear it for . . . Sheffield United!' I yelled.

Uproar, verging on hysteria.

'Let's hear it for . . . Sean Bean!'

Cheering.

'Let's hear it for . . . *The Full Monty*!'

Dead loud cheering.

'Let's hear it for . . . ' I paused to steady myself, my brain quickly running out of ideas. 'Let's hear it for . . . cutlery!'

That got a laugh. Someone from the crowd shouted out a suggestion. 'OK,' I agreed, 'but only cos I'm feeling magnmi . . . magmani . . . generous. Let's hear it for . . . Sheffield Wednesday!' A muted response, with some polite applause from the rear.

Gathering the lead from my microphone, I prepared to launch into my first number. 'Trev—the drums, please!' I was rewarded with a spotlight, centre right. 'And now, beginning with that old classic from Oasis . . . "She's electric . . . She's electric . . . She's in a family full of eccentrics . . . "'

'Suzanne!'

'" . . . she's done things I never expected and I need more time . . . "'

'Suzanne!'

'"She's got a brother . . . we don't get on with one another but I quite fancy her mother . . . "'

'Suzanne! Get down now!'

Dimly, I registered that someone was shouting my name. I twirled round to where Dad was standing in the spotlight, which I realized was actually light from the hallway, but I chose to pretend otherwise. I held out my arms, beseeching him to join me on stage. 'Ladies and gentleman,' I announced, 'I give you . . . Geoff Fish!' I pointed the microphone towards him, whispering that he'd have to change his name if he wanted more street cred.

'No, Suzanne! Not one more word out of you, is that clear?'

I gawped at him in surprise. Something in the tone of his voice penetrated my thick skull. There was a hard edge to it, like when teachers have been pushed too far. I wobbled. The whole arena was hushed, waiting . . . He twisted his head briefly, shouting into the hallway for Chris to fetch the ladder. I glanced over the side of Old Bluey. It was a long drop.

'Come one step closer and I'll jump!' I joked.

'Shut up!'

'Dad!'

'Shut up!'

I found it difficult to take in the order and the venom with which it was delivered. My brain searched rapidly for some explanation. That wasn't my dad, not my dad. Only dads with brown teeth and bad breath spoke to their kids like that.

Chris emerged, soundlessly placing the ladder against the ambulance, holding it steady as I fumbled my way downwards. 'Don't say anything, just go straight to bed,' he whispered.

'Why?'

'Christ, Sue, you know what he's like about drinking . . . '

'I only had semon lodas!' I protested, flouncing past him and into the hall. 'Dad!' I called. 'I only had semon lodas!'

Dad had his arm outstretched, barring my way upstairs. His eyes forbade me to move. Narrowed and dark, like shellfish retreating into themselves, they pierced me, pinning me to the spot. 'Don't even think about going upstairs with that child asleep up there,' he hissed.

59

'I wasn't . . . I just wanted . . . '

'Where have you been?' he demanded.

There seemed little point in lying. 'To a pub,' I said with rapidly fading bravado.

'That much I know! That much is obvious!'

'I'm sorry I'm late . . . I did phone . . . didn't Sam tell you?'

'Look at you! Standing there—reeking of beer and smoke—your make-up smeared all over your face.'

I opened my mouth to speak but nothing emerged. I was still rooted to his shellfish eyes. And petrified.

'How old are you?' he bellowed.

'Sixteen.'

'Sixteen! And it's legal to drink at sixteen now, is it?'

'No,' I whispered.

'No, I didn't think so. And were you raped on the way home, you stupid girl?'

'No! I . . . '

'How would you know? How would you stop it?' he asked icily.

Chris interrupted then, stepping forward from the front door where he had been standing, hands sunk into pockets, eyes examining the carpet. 'I think you're a bit out of order now, Pops,' he said quietly. Dad swivelled round to say something but Chris straightened up, staring him out.

'I'm sorry,' I said to them both, 'I'm sorry.'

Dad's face seemed to crumple then. 'Go to your room,' he said, his voice expressionless.

I climbed the stairs in a trance, thankful to escape the stranger with tears in his eyes.

I must have zonked out immediately. When I came round, it was pitch black and someone was snoring on the floor next to me. I tried to sit up but the effort was too much and I sank back into my pillow. 'Is that you, Jimmy?' I asked, confused, then realized what I was

60

saying. The snores increased in depth and pace, followed by a loud, contented fart. 'Chris?' I mumbled.

Tentatively I reached out and shook him. 'Chris?'

'What?' he muttered.

'Why are you sleeping on my bedroom floor?'

'In case you do a Hendrix on us.'

'Eh?'

'Choke to death on your own spew.'

'Oh, charming.'

He groaned as I switched on my table lamp. 'Chris, I feel a mess.'

'You will do, you've got a hangover, you daft bint!'

'No,' I wailed, 'I mean it. I think I've done it in my jeans.'

'Oh, great!'

Without another word, my guardian angel gathered up his bedding and returned to his room. I staggered to the bathroom, where things were not too disgusting but still bad enough. I rinsed my pants and jeans out in the shower then stuffed them into the linen basket. Then I tried to be sick again but nothing would come. I knew I ought to put my fingers down my throat but I couldn't face it. I could never be a bulimic.

Back in my room, I stripped off the rest of my clothes and groped for my T-shirt. I felt cold and shivery. It was only five o'clock but I couldn't get back to sleep. I lay there, listless and nauseous, flinching every time I remembered what I'd done and said.

'Good night out, honey?' James Dean asked mockingly.

'Drop dead!'

'I did.'

I dozed fitfully, my foot jerking out every few minutes as scenes jumped into my head like a demonic slide projector. 'And here's one where you phoned Lee and told him you loved him.' Oh no. 'And this is the one where you are telling the girls all about Karenna.' Oh no. 'And here's the one where you climbed on to the ambulance and . . . here's your dad turning into a bastard.' Oh, no, no, no!

I tensed as my bedroom door was pushed open, breathing out with relief when I saw it was Mum. 'How are you?' she asked gently, holding out a glass of water towards me.

I took delicate sips like a Victorian heroine on her death-bed. 'I think I've got flu,' I said pitifully.

'It's called flu when you phone in to work ill, it's called a hangover when you're amongst friends.'

My eyes filled with prickly tears. 'Dad . . . ' I began.

'I know,' she said, brushing my hair away from my face, 'I heard—Chris told me. Don't take it to heart, love. You gave him a big shock—you're his princess, remember?'

'Not any more, I'm not.'

She sighed heavily, glancing at her watch. 'I wish I wasn't working, we could do with a long talk. Look, Geoff's going to Grandma's this morning. If I were you I'd stay in bed until he's gone then clean up a bit. Use your own judgement on how to take it from there. He might just want to forget it, you know what he's like.'

I pictured again the shellfish eyes. 'No, I don't,' I said. 'I thought I did but I don't.'

'Don't be melodramatic. You're well aware of your father's aversion to alcohol. What did you expect? Now, make sure you drink as much water as you can to stop you becoming dehydrated,' she advised.

'Yes, nurse,' I mumbled.

'And try to be sick. It'll get all the poison out of your system.'

'What poison? I was only drinking cocktails, not arsenic.'

'Alcohol is a poison, Suzanne, especially on an empty stomach. Next time, eat before you go out drinking, don't mix your drink, and have water in-between.'

'Next time? There won't be a next time!' I said

vehemently, groaning as a spasm of nausea bolted across my guts.

Mum pointed to the water again. 'That's what they all say.' She frowned, as if working something out. 'I suppose you hardly ever see us drinking socially, so you don't know how to do it properly.'

'Patchouli warned me about the Knock-outs but I didn't take any notice.'

'Did she? That was sensible of her.'

'And she and Zoe brought me home.'

'Then you should be grateful. Anything can happen when you're drunk and alone—male or female. Just drop in to casualty one Friday or Saturday night—you'll see. Your father's right in that sense.'

'I know, I know. Give me a break.'

'I will but we'll need to talk about this when you've got rid of your hangover.'

'It's flu!' I said, turning away.

10

I did as suggested and waited until I heard Old Bluey
wheeze into life before going downstairs. Chris was in
the kitchen, stuffing Weetabix down his neck and
reading the papers. 'Do we have to have that on?' I
asked feebly, staring at the CD player.

He glanced up, smirking. 'Thought you'd like it—it's
your debut album.'

'Ha, ha,' I said, using all my energy to turn down the
volume on 'She's electric'. Slowly, I lowered myself on
to the chair opposite him. 'How long will I feel like
this?' I groaned.

Chris stared into my eyes for a second, then helped
himself to more Weetabix. 'What were you on?' he
asked.

'Knock-outs.'

'Ah, "Semon Lodas". Cocktails are fatal. Stick to beer.'

I slumped forward, resting my head in my arms. 'I
want to die,' I said.

'So, come on, what else did you do on your first
bingeing session, apart from knacker the roof of Dad's
van? Reveal all.'

'I told Lee Anderson I loved him.'

'He has my deepest sympathy.'

'Stop it, my life's over.'

'Why?'

Briefly, and because I was too tired not to, I explained
all about Lee. My brother, my confidant, snorted.

'I'll never be able to look him in the face again,' I
said, hurt.

''Course you will. He's not going to mention it, is he? He's a bloke.'

'It's all right for you; you're as good as married. I can't even ask somebody out without the aid of chemical substances. I'll have put him right off.'

'Maybe, but if it doesn't the next problem you've got is whether he's thinking about his ex when he's necking you. Take it from one who's been there, done it, bought the T-shirt with "Rebound Boy" on it.'

I'd read enough problem pages in my life to recognize common sense when I heard it. With great reluctance, I had to admit Chris might be right. Lee had been pretty cut up all week about Billy-Jo, though I had pretended otherwise. The old denial setting in again. I struggled to hold back the tears. 'I don't stand a chance with him anyway, girlfriend or no girlfriend. He just sees me as a boff,' I sniffled.

'He said he'd sit with you, didn't he?' Chris reminded me.

'Probably just wants to ask me about combustion,' I pouted miserably.

Chris began to get exasperated. 'OK, so he says no, so what? What's the worst thing that can happen? You learn from rejection, Miss Counsellor. Actually, it might do you good to fail at something once in your life,' he said seriously.

'Meaning?'

'Meaning you'd do anything to avoid people not liking you.' He launched into his take-the-mick routine. ' "Babysit Sam, Suzanne, even though I'm the parent and should be doing it." " 'Course I will." "Be a Star Mentor and save me doing playground duty, Suzanne." " 'Course I will." "Take maths a year early to make the school look good." " 'Course I will." "Offer Chris your bedroom to play Happy Families— 'course I will." '

I jolted upright angrily, my head throbbing. 'It's called helping people. Not that you'd know anything about that!'

Chris belched and pushed his cereal bowl away. 'Getting crocked last night was the first genuine thing you've ever done in your life.'

'Get stuffed! I feel lousy and all you can do is slag me off. At least I'm honest about my drinking—I don't pretend I've never touched a drop in my life like some people.'

My brother shrugged. 'I might push my luck sometimes but I'm not that thick.' My eyes launched a battalion of daggers in the stirrer's direction but they landed in no-man's land. It wasn't fair. Hangovers really limit your debating powers.

'I'll probably be grounded for life!' I said beginning to feel really sorry for myself.

Chris laughed so loud I could see tiny heaps of claggy cereal stuck to his fillings. 'Oh, right!' he said contemptuously. 'As if he'll say a thing to the Gifted One. He'll just pretend it never happened, like he does whenever anything uncomfortable happens to shake him out of his cosy world; like his redundancy or Mum's post-natal depression or his sordid childhood.'

'What do you mean? He had a normal childhood.'

'Ask him.'

'Tell me!'

Frustratingly, Chris pointed to the United report. 'Another spawny result for your lot, I notice.'

I blanked my rat of a sibling out, fixing my eyes on the microwave behind his head. He talked cobblers.

From the hallway came the terrifying sound of the phone ringing. I stared at Chris, willing him to answer but he was ignoring it deliberately. Slowly, I made my way to the instrument of torture. What if it was Lee asking for an explanation? I'd almost rather it was Karenna than Lee. 'Hello?' I whispered hoarsely.

'Fishy?' Patchouli asked.

'Hi.'

'Feeling rough?'

'Not many.'

'What did your dad say?'

I cleared my throat. 'Nothing much.'

'Look, we're really sorry we didn't take you to your door—it's one of our rules and we broke it.'

'I was home in two minutes.'

'Do you remember everything?'

'Unfortunately.'

'We need to have big words about Sheldon. Why don't you come down to our house later on?'

I mumbled some feeble excuse.

'OK, but you're not ducking out of it, Sue. I mean it—you've got to get rid of her.'

'What, assassinate her, you mean?'

'No, you know what I mean—get rid of her from your subconscious.'

'Mmm,' I mmm'd. She had definitely watched even more Oprahs than I had.

'Gorra go, Fishy. See you in prison Monday— maybe.'

'Yeah, see you.'

Chris ambled into the hallway and yanked his jacket off the banister rail. 'The love interest?' he asked.

'Patchouli,' I replied absently.

He grimaced. 'What were her parents on when they named her?'

'Well, not a donkey like yours!'

'Ooh. So droll. I must away to a six-bedroomed Edwardian villa on the Eccleshall Road to escape your rapier-like tongue.'

'I'm going to bed,' I announced.

'I'd do a machine wash first, if I were you. You don't want Dad finding your jeans,' he said, sounding as if he cared.

Instant barbecued cheeks. 'Oh. Oh, don't remind me.'

He opened the front door, sending me reeling from the blast of freezing air. 'I'll never mention it again,' he lied, then bellowed, 'Let's hear it for cutlery!' at the top of his voice before disappearing.

Squeamishly, I sloped upstairs to fetch the dreaded linen basket and prepared to get rid of the evidence of the most 'genuine thing' I'd ever done in my life.

Mrs Parminter had taught us a technique called 'Fogging' in PSRE. Fogging can help if you are being slagged off. If someone says 'You're dead ugly, you are', you reply to the person 'Am I?' or 'I agree' but inside you say to yourself, 'No, I'm not, I'm ace.'

As I loaded the washing machine, I thought about what Chris had said, that I'd do anything to avoid rejection. 'No I wouldn't,' I fogged to myself. But there was no fog. Not even a slight mist. Despising him for it, I had to admit he was right. Fear of rejection, low self-esteem, denial—all the familiar chat-show words came tumbling down, sticking to me like Velcroed labels. And now I'd ended up blowing any chance with Lee. I knew I wouldn't fancy anyone who called me up when they were blathered. 'Call him now, then,' my brain ordered. 'Later,' I begged. I set the machine on non-fast coloureds and retreated to the front room.

After turning the gas fire up full blast I curled up on the settee. Chris's words had affected me powerfully, as had Patchouli's last night. My mind juggled with itself, shooting questions out like some manic self-service lie-detector.

'Why did you become a mentor?'

'To help others.'

'Beep! Try again.'

'To help kids avoid going through what I went through?'

'Close.'

My eyes began to prickle. My throat felt like hardened chamois leather when I tried to swallow.

'To get rid of Karenna.'

'Yes! Spot on! Well done! Did it work?'

'A bit.'

'Did it work?'

'Leave me alone.'

'Did it work?'

'No.'

'Thank you. Next question. Why don't you believe in yourself?'

'What do you mean?'

'Not believing you have natural intelligence, for instance. Always apologizing for being a "boff" like last night with Patchouli.'

'I haven't got natural intelligence—it's forced from the time with Karenna.'

'Who told you . . . ?'

'Who told me I was thick.'

'So you . . . '

'So I worked like mad in lessons to prove her wrong and asked for extra work to make up for always being away.'

'And you still work hard to prove her wrong even though she's gone or had gone. Why?'

'It pleased everybody.'

'Especially at home.'

'Yes,' I agreed.

'Because when Mum came home exhausted from shift work and Dad was frustrated from no work and Chris was failing his exams and Sammy was demanding everyone's attention you thought you should be the one to provide that one constant light in the home, didn't you?'

'That was how it seemed, yes.'

'You can see a pattern developing, here, can't you, Suzanne?'

'Yes.'

'What are you going to do?'

'Put the wash on spin.'

I drooped into the kitchen, mechanically twisting the dial to 'S'. I felt drained and tearful, my mind reeling, ready to combust, as it tried to decipher a thousand conversations at once. Combust . . . combustion! A giant light bulb suddenly flashed across my brain, zapping me with the words 'test' and 'tomorrow'. Problem solved, *merci beaucoups*. I had revision to do for an important test. Everything else could wait. Or preferably go away. Sorted!

But upstairs in my bedroom, my chemistry notes in neat sections waiting to be highlighted, re-drafted, and memorized, I knew something had changed. I tried putting it down to the hangover, thinking the alcohol had done swinish things to my thought processes. Sentences began normally enough: 'When energy is released in a chemical reaction there is a rise in temperature—this is called . . . *Karenna Sheldon* . . . ' I tried again. 'If the energy released when forming new bonds is greater than the energy needed to break existing bonds this causes . . . *a need to talk to your father.*'

'Want my advice, baby?' James Dean asked.

I stared hard at my fantasy male, sitting on his director's chair, calm and poised and handsome, waiting to die. I felt turned-on, as I always did, when I imagined what it must have been like to make love to him. But I did not respond to his question today. Almost imperceptibly, James Dean became my James Dean poster, frayed at the edges, lumpy at the back from too much Blu-Tack.

Beneath my window, Old Bluey grunted on to the driveway. I heard Sam yelling to Dad to watch him jump the steps. I bundled my chem notes into my folder and went downstairs.

70

11

Dad and I had never had an argument—I know that sounds impossible but it's true. Maybe we were unusual—the Bisto family Lyndsay teased me about— but every family was different and I couldn't help it if mine was OK.

Dad once told me that when he took me for my injections as a baby he used to feel physical pain when the needle went in, and if he could have, he'd have had the injection for me. I always remembered that—it helped me a lot through the bad times, knowing he loved me so much.

I realized now my drunken state must have caused him physical pain, but it had liberated me. Not that I was stupid enough to think alcohol was going to solve any of my problems and I definitely wasn't going to go berserk with cocktails next time, but I knew there would be a next time.

My shock and humiliation at Dad's reaction had dissolved into embarrassment but I would not ignore it. Until I straightened things with him, I couldn't straighten the rest of my world—with Lee or Karenna. Especially with Karenna. I sat on the bottom step and waited for him to come in.

Only Sam entered, grabbing my hand and pulling me into the kitchen. 'Look where I hidded your biscuit,' he said, proud of his inventiveness.

'Where?'

'In here, so Chris wouldn't eat it.' From beneath a bag of garden peas in the freezer, Sam retrieved

71

his offering, blowing ice particles from the midget gems.

'That looks . . . cool!' I laughed. 'I can't wait to have it with my tea.' To prove it, I placed it reverently on to one of our best plates, next to the pot I had brewed for Dad and me. 'Is there another one for Daddy?' I asked.

Sam shook his head solemnly, 'No. He ate his yesterday. I'm going to make a house for Robin Hood and his Many Men. Do you want to help me?' he said, already halfway out of the kitchen.

'I want to talk to Dad first,' I replied. 'Where is he?'

'In the garage. I have to be good and leave him alone.'

'You don't always have to be good,' I called after him.

My hands began to sweat slightly as I loaded a tray with my cargo and prepared to meet the man with shellfish eyes.

He was kneeling down beside a dining room chair, measuring the seat frame. I stood uncertainly by the open mouth of the garage, watching him concentrate on the wooden carcass. The tray began to weigh heavily. 'I've brought you a cup of tea,' I said in a small voice.

Dad glanced up briefly, then returned to the chair. 'Thanks, pet. Leave it on the drawers,' he replied casually, normally.

I entered the garage, sliding the tray on to the drawers which had once been in my old bedroom but which Dad now kept all his tools inside.

The words I wanted to say stuck in my throat like dry tablets. Instead I watched, as the upholsterer deftly slotted the loose seat, newly covered in a rich blue damask, back into place. Behind him, its three partners, already complete, nodded in silent admiration.

'They're nice,' I ventured. 'Who are they for?'

'Oh, a woman on Portland Street,' he replied, frowning at the last chair. Shaking his head, he removed the seat again, flipping it upside down, searching for faults.

'Dad.'

'Mmm?'

'About last night . . . '

He didn't look up. 'Forget it.'

'I can't,' I said. 'I need to talk to you about it.'

'There's always one that won't lie true,' he muttered, addressing the seat.

'I'm sorry I was drunk,' I pursued.

There was a long sigh. 'Well, it won't happen again, will it?' he said, wrapping the rogue chair seat in polythene. 'Least said, soonest mended, eh?'

He caught my eye, then. No shellfish—just pleading.

It would have been the easiest thing in the world to agree, to do a Princess Suzanne and promise to be good. Instead I reached for his beaker and took it to him. 'I was stupid,' I admitted. 'I drank too much, too fast.'

He accepted the tea, not quite looking directly at me this time. 'And I'm . . . I'm sorry for reacting the way I did. I . . . ' he faltered.

'I understand,' I interrupted. 'I know it must have been a shock. I bet I looked a right idiot but . . . '

Dad smiled with relief, believing he was back on planet Days-gone-by with his angelic daughter. 'Well, I'll just sort this job out then get dinner ready. Your mum will be home any minute and . . . '

'I probably will drink again, though, Dad,' I said hurriedly. 'I enjoyed it. I could let myself go. It made me question things that—'

'Suzanne!' he snapped. 'You're too young, you're under age.'

'Dad, I'm at least two years behind most of my friends. If taking drink and drugs were on the curriculum I'd be special needs!'

His mouth set in a hard, firm line. 'No, Suzanne, you will not go out to pubs. It's a destructive . . . damaging

73

. . . addictive . . . ' He became agitated, pacing the garage floor, slopping tea over the edge of his beaker.

I felt sorry for him, wanted to reassure him that I'd handle the drink better next time. 'Why do you hate alcohol so much? Is it because of Grandad?' I blurted.

'Never mind,' he said shortly.

'Was Grandad an alcoholic?' I persisted.

'No.'

'Dad, please. How am I going to learn if you don't teach me anything?'

He seemed flabbergasted. 'Learn? Learn from that bastard?'

I opened my eyes wide in shock. Dad hardly ever swore and then only at inanimate objects such as politicians. He saw my reaction and sighed deeply, then sank on to the plastic covered chair nearby. I leaned against the drawers and waited, my heart beating rapidly in anticipation. Breakthrough.

Staring at the concrete floor, Dad began. 'My father . . . wasn't an alcoholic in that he hid whisky bottles in the airing cupboard—that sort of thing. He was like a lot of working men in those days. He broke his back all day in the foundry and expected something in return. To him, that was a couple of pints on the way home, his dinner on the table, then out again for a few more jars.'

'Every night?'

'More or less, depending on the shift and if the money was there. He drank away most of his wages.'

I knew the feeling, remembering my dismay at the cost of my round in The Bricklayer's Arms. 'What did Gran do?' I asked, probing further.

'What could she do? She didn't expect anything different—most women didn't then.'

'He did love her, though, didn't he?'

Dad shrugged. 'As long as his Yorkshire's were on the table and his shirts were ironed he loved her, though he had a funny way of showing it at times.'

'Why? He didn't hit her, did he?'

74

I waited for him to reply. He had only ever told me odd things now and again from his childhood, about fishing and school. It had all seemed normal—boring even—until now. Dad took a slow sip of his tea. 'Oh, he hit her all right. He used his fists and she retaliated with anything she could lay her hands on—pokers, frying pans—you name it, she used it!'

That was OK, then. I had this picture of her chasing him round the table like in a Charlie Chaplin film shouting, 'I'll teach you to come home in this state, Leonard Fish!' 'So she gave as good as she got,' I smiled, 'that's my gran!'

Dad glared at me angrily. 'Of course she didn't! He was built like a barn door, for heaven's sake. He broke her jaw more than once.'

'That's awful!' I felt a sudden hatred for this man I had never seen. Shame, too, that he was part of my family. 'What did you do?'

I saw a little boy like Sam, dressed in grey flannel shorts and a Fair Isle tank top, watching the fights, terrified out of his wits.

'Janet and I used to hide in the cupboard under the stairs, waiting until the noise stopped.'

'I wish I'd been there. I'd have sorted him out,' I said.

He digested this idea, continuing thoughtfully, 'Yes, maybe you would, Suzanne. You're a lot more confident than I was—a lot more aware of what abuse is, with your newspaper cuttings and that. Maybe if I'd been a bit braver I could have spared Mum some of her beatings. I often dreamed of killing him, or at least giving him a taste of his own medicine, but I never did . . . I just walked out the minute I could, when I was fifteen.'

I gazed blindly at my feet, feeling angry with myself for my tactless comment. 'I would have sorted him out.' Yeah—just like I sorted out Sheldon. Chris was right. I was like my dad, but that didn't make either of us bad or

75

weak, just unarmed. Neither of us stood a chance on our own—we were too young, for a start, the enemy too powerful. We needed help, but Dad didn't get it and I hadn't sought it.

'Did it help when he died?' I asked, presuming it had.

He shook his head. 'No, because I never tackled him about it—even when he was an old man, dying in that clinic, fit for nothing. I never said, "Aren't you sorry for what you did?" And at the funeral, when everyone was going on about what a grand bloke old Len was, how the true measure of a man was whether he stood his round in a pub or not, and Len was one of the truest, I smiled and agreed with them, thinking "What does that make me, then?" So no, it didn't help when he died, it made it worse, because I can never bring it to a close. All I can do . . . ' he laughed bitterly at himself. 'All I can do is terrify my daughter when she starts acting her age.'

'Oh, Dad!' I rushed across to hug him. 'I understand, honest. I know just how you feel.'

'I doubt that you do, love, thank God,' he replied, ruffling my hair. We held each other for a few seconds, then Dad asked if I minded him being left alone for a bit.

I obeyed, knowing he needed space to think. I hoped he wasn't in the dark cupboard any more.

Later, after Sam had gone to bed, Dad opened up to all of us about his childhood. Chris and I bombarded him with questions while Mum sat there, shaking her head and sympathizing with Gran. 'And it still goes on, you know, domestic violence. People thinking they've got the right to lash at someone just because they live under the same roof. Society hasn't made much progress, has it?' she asked.

Dad rubbed his bristly chin thoughtfully. 'Oh, I don't know. Hospitals and schools seem to question suspicious injuries a lot more now—they never did back then. Our doctor must have known what was going on when I took my mother in with one broken bone after another. He never said a word. My teacher was no better with my bruises. "Been fighting with walls again, Geoffrey?" he'd say, knowing full well what had gone off.'

'It wasn't your fault, you know, Dad. None of it,' Chris said quietly, staring into the fire.

'No, well, at least I can take credit for not passing his bad temper on to the next generation. I always vowed I'd never raise a hand to my children and I never have.'

'Suzanne could have done with a slap from time to time to knock some of that cockiness out of her,' Chris teased.

I gave him a swift kick. 'Get lost!'

Dad laughed and hugged my shoulders. 'No way. Not my prin—, not my daughter.'

Ah, Bisto!

12

Monday morning. Porker, our bus driver, slammed on his brakes and swerved into a lay-by, shouting up to the psychos on the top deck to sit down or he'd kick their heads in. Sadly, the psychos were too busy stuffing sports bags through the emergency exit to hear.

I sat, patiently waiting for the ritual to end so I could get to school. Actually, I was relieved; the later the bus was, the longer I postponed seeing Lee in chemistry. I cringed every time I thought about my slurred declarations of love on Saturday. My hangover might have worn off but I was still feeling the repercussions.

We had parked opposite the Piazza. Despite myself, I glanced across at Snippits where there appeared to be little activity. Funny how only nine days ago that salon meant nothing to me—it was just a boring little shop set amongst other boring little shops on the way to school. Now though, I knew what happened behind that plate-glass door. I knew where the coffee was kept and how to fluff the towels so they looked as if they'd been washed when they hadn't. I knew which customers wanted *Hello!* to read and which wanted *Family Circle*. I knew Karenna Sheldon was the junior stylist.

'You've got to get rid of her.' Patchouli's impassioned words rang in my ears. Silently, I acknowledged that she was right. Even if I had never set foot in Snippits, never met Karenna again during the rest of my life, she would always be there, gnawing away at the fragile part of me that needed to be free. What I didn't want was to be like my dad, missing the chance to close the circle, to make

78

myself whole. Coincidence or fate or something had conspired that Karenna and I should meet again. I knew I would be returning to Snippits at least one more time.

Porker, meanwhile, satisfied that his bus was now fit to drive, even if he wasn't, slammed into gear and headed for Steetley.

Mr West opened the lab door and generously invited us in. The test papers were laid out ready and waiting. As usual, I sat behind Kevin and Lee. 'You have all lesson,' Mr West informed us, 'so don't rush and always . . . ' He paused, eyebrows raised.

'Read the question,' we chanted unanimously.

'Ah, I adore top sets,' Mr West sighed, settling down to an hour of well-deserved marking.

I tried to focus on the paper but my eyes kept drifting to Lee's back. Chris had warned me he wouldn't say anything but I had hoped for some small gesture—a dirty look, a shrug, an engagement ring—to reciprocate my drunken disclosure. What I got was a folded note which had been secreted between page 1: Exothermic Reactions and page 2: something blurry.

The note was simple and straight to the point. 'I'm back with Billy-Jo—thought you might want to know.' A poem! Short but not sweet and, deep-down, not unexpected. I re-read the note wishing emotions were easier to handle. Emotions, I reckoned, should be kept in a golden envelope, safe and sealed, so that they could be presented to the Chosen One to be looked after properly. If the Chosen One did not wish to receive your envelope, it should be kept safe anyway, sacred and undamaged, ready for next time. I'd had my envelope returned, slightly torn but otherwise intact. The rejection stung, but not as much as I thought it would, and Lee had let me down easy, in a safe, non-committed way. So, there would be no romantic night of passion in a minibus but I was still lovely and tall and a guy with a sharp haircut had grinned at me in The Bricklayer's Arms. Positive thoughts, Suzanne. Positive thoughts. I closed my eyes for a second, cleared my throat, picked up my pen, and began to write.

'How did you do on that one?' Lee asked at the end as he always does.

I gave him a faint smile, grateful he was being normal. 'Not brilliant,' I replied.

'Oh, yeah—as if!' Kevin Cooper said sarcastically.

'I didn't,' I protested, 'but I'll still have done really OK.'

'Big-head.'

For once, I was not prepared to be put-down or put myself down. 'No, I'm not a big-head, I just know I'm brainy and it's OK to be brainy,' I replied seriously.

He seemed lost for an answer.

Lee thumped Cooper's back, hard. 'The girl's right, Kevvo; it's OK to be brainy . . . and cool with it.' He steered his mate towards the door, grinning at me. A friendly grin. An 'I don't fancy you but you're sound' grin.

'Say "hi" to Billy-Jo,' I called after him. I don't know whether he heard or not, he was too busy assuring Kevin that yes, he thought he was brainy and cool with it, too.

Outside, the early spring wind scattered crisp packets across the playground as I began my tour of duty. Lyndsay had a dental appointment and wasn't coming in to school until lunchtime, which was a relief for me if not her.

Her absence gave me a chance to do the job properly without distractions. I disagreed with Lyndsay and Chris's view on mentoring being 'sad'. Maybe I had entered into it for the wrong reasons but I still thought it was an important thing for our school to have—a step in the right direction.

80

A minute later my heart sank as Mr Penny, hands clasped around his mug of tea, made a reluctant appearance on to the tarmac. He must have swapped duties.

At once, a gang of about five kids ran to him, pointing and shouting towards the huts. 'There's a fight, Mr Penny—a right scrap!' He shooed them away impatiently and walked in the opposite direction. Typical!

Behind hut two, Kyle Smith had Edwin Gurney, a new boy, pinned against the damp bargeboards. Around them, Kyle's cronies bayed for blood. Edwin, a small, timid kid who smelt of urine and spent a lot of time 'helping' the librarians, looked petrified as the much stronger Kyle, his knuckled fist clamped against Edwin's throat, threatened to 'deck' him.

'What's going on?' I demanded.

Kyle, a known hard case, glanced at me angrily. 'He started it.'

'Save it till later, Kyle. Let him go.' Kyle, remembering he was a gnat's hair away from suspension, dropped Edwin instantly so that he stumbled into the rubble.

'Disappear then,' I ordered the audience. Kyle tried to join them. 'Not you—you know the rules.' The rules were the mentor had to report any aggravation to the teacher on duty who then filled out an incident report. Penny, true to form, took the easy way out when I presented him with the Disparate Duo.

'Well, there doesn't seem to be any need for first-aid, Samantha, does there?' he said.

'Kyle was using threatening behaviour—he broke the code of conduct,' I pointed out, knowing to correct my name was only wasting time.

'It was nowt, sir, just a bit of messing around,' Smith blustered, using the time-honoured cliché.

'N-no you wasn't,' Edwin stammered, his eyes bright with tears he was desperately trying to hold back. A bubble of mucus dangled repulsively from his nose.

'Go and play properly, the pair of you,' Penny ordered, dismissing them with a wave of his hand, 'and get a tissue or something, you filthy child!' he snapped at Edwin. Kyle belted off in triumph, yelling to his prey he'd see him at dinner. Edwin edged closer to me and I felt for his hand and held it fast. The teacher dunked his tea bag yet again, waiting for us to disappear.

I think it was that that did it; the constant dipping in and out, as if nothing else in the world mattered to this man except the strength of his hot drink. Penny was totally oblivious to the boy shaking with misery in front of him, just as he'd been totally oblivious to me five years previously. Maybe, just maybe, if he'd helped me that day, I could have been spared a few months of unhappiness. Well, it was not going to happen to Edwin, too. 'Are you going to fill out an incident form?' I asked Mr Penny brusquely.

He looked at his watch and shrugged. 'Mmm? No, I haven't time for all that.'

All that rubbish he meant. He might as well go up to Edwin at lunchtime and give him a kicking himself. I glared into the teacher's indifferent eyes, making up my mind suddenly. 'I think you ought to know I'm reporting you for neglecting children's rights. You're a crap teacher, Mr Penny—you always have been and you always will be!' I stormed off, my hands shaking as much as Edwin's as I headed towards Mrs Parminter's office. I heard a faint 'What?' from behind as my words registered and hit home.

Mrs Parminter just looked stunned by the time I had finished my tirade against her head of art. 'Well,' she said, pushing her specs more comfortably up the bridge of her nose, 'I shall certainly be taking this further, Suzanne. Everyone should be following the code of conduct at Steetley, including members of staff but . . . ' she hesitated, taking time to end her sentence. 'But you'll appreciate I have to be careful how I tackle this, especially as you were rude. Will you leave it with me?'

I nodded. I trusted Mrs Parminter. I knew she'd say something to Mr Penny. I knew he'd deny it totally but that didn't matter. I'd made my point.

I was about to leave when she called me back, catching me out with the million dollar question. 'I know you take your mentoring seriously, Suzanne, but I've never seen you this animated and upset. Is there more to this you're not telling me?'

I hesitated, tempted to tell her about my life here before she arrived, but I didn't. I couldn't risk it getting back to Mum and Dad and Chris. Zoe and Patch had reacted badly enough to my tale of woe; it would devastate my family to know they hadn't been there for me, especially Dad, so who would benefit? No one. One day, in my own time, maybe, I'd tell them. Not yet.

I met my headteacher's enquiring gaze with a challenge. 'Ask around, Mrs Parminter. Ask the kids. They'll tell you who the good teachers are and the bad ones. You're always saying we need to listen to the children. Do it then!'

'Yes,' she said, smiling apologetically, 'I know.'

Outside the office, a bashful Edwin handed me a squashed KitKat. 'Thanks, Suzanne,' he said shyly.

'Any time,' I smiled.

13

For once, the climb up Roman Hill after school did not seem like an endurance test. The days were lengthening now, and the creamy sun warmed my face as I paused at the top to catch my breath. Ahead of me, the road disappeared down to Brightside and eventually led on to the domed shopper's paradise of Meadowhall which had replaced the steelworks where my dad and my grandad used to work.

Lulled by the milder weather, I parked myself on the grass and focused on the distant motorway traffic. A feeling of tranquillity settled within me as I watched lane after lane of cars file sluggishly across each other in the tea-time congestion. I was grateful I did not have to jump into a tiny metal machine and battle alongside hundreds of other machines to get home.

I thought about James Dean dying when he was only twenty-four, his beautiful neck snapped in half. Indulgent tears jabbed at my eyes. Then, without warning, I visualized little Edwin Gurney, his face bleached white as Smith prepared to batter him. Edwin's face suddenly turned into my dad's as a boy, equally as terrified, but in shadow as he fumbled to close the cupboard door. Tears were falling freely down my face now, as the cupboard changed into the school bog, and there was I, crouching down, retrieving my sandwiches for Karenna.

And just as suddenly as they had started, the tears stopped. It wasn't twelve-year-old Suzanne Fish who gazed meekly back at Karenna. It was the new girl—the one who was almost a woman. She was lovely and tall and not afraid any more. The new girl had faith in herself and that was all she had ever needed.

I stood up, brushing damp grass from my trousers, feeling . . . feeling strong. I had already been strong enough to face up to my dad after Saturday and to deal with my feelings for Lee. I had also been strong enough to tell Mrs Parminter a member of her staff was useless. Now I knew I was strong enough to go to Snippits next Saturday.

Adrenalin surged through me as I remembered my night out with Patchouli and Zoe. They had been real friends, interested in me, looking out for me, as well as being nutters with it. Lyndsay would probably have shoved me in the taxi alone and carried on doing her own thing. I shook my head ruefully and decided if Ms Fritton wanted my friendship she was going to have to work a bit harder for it from now on.

I sang 'She's electric' at the top of my voice all the way home and would have jumped on to Old Bluey again for a return performance, had Dad not driven her off somewhere.

Upstairs, the landing was in chaos. Sam was dragging his duvet into the study, a look of grim determination on his sweated brow. On the carpet were scattered an assortment of pieces of jigsaw, books, biscuits, and clothes. 'What's going on?' I asked.

The labourer paused for a brief second to speak. 'Hi, Suzanne. Guess what? I'm moving rooms. It was doing my legs in sharing with Chris so I'm having the study. I know it's small but I'll have my own space. Then I can impress myself.'

'Express yourself,' I corrected, wondering immediately where the computer was going—one of the reasons we had created the 'study'—a poky room next to the bathroom little bigger than a walk-in wardrobe—was so the computer would be on neutral territory. Chris and I both used it mega-amounts.

Mum stuck her head round the ex-study door, her face flushed from re-assembling Sam's bed. 'Hi, love.'

'Hi.'

'I never learn, do I?' she smiled. 'One day, a day off will mean a day off.'

'Computer in Chris's room?' I asked. She nodded apologetically and I headed straight in to claim visitation rights.

Chris was lying on his bed, half-dressed in only T-shirt and boxer shorts, a smug look on his face.

'Sam said you were doing his legs in!' I informed him cheerfully.

He grinned. 'Ah, Sam, that sweet little scallywag. How is he these days?'

I did a swift reccy, locating the computer in the space where the scallywag's bed had been. 'You'd better let me use it when I need to,' I warned.

'No problem,' said the newly-liberated one. 'How was chemistry?'

'I'll probably only get a B.'

'I meant with that guy.'

'Oh, he's back with Billy-Jo,' I said matter-of-factly.

'You OK?'

I stared at Chris, waiting for the sarky punchline but he seemed genuinely concerned. 'I'm fine.'

'Honestly?'

'Honestly. It would never have worked out anyway. I think I only liked him because he was always unavailable.'

'Like James Dean?'

'Yeah, like James Dean, only less dead!' I smiled, trying to work out when Chris had stopped treating me like a kid sister. Probably around the time Dad had stopped calling me 'princess'. I remembered how Chris had protected me from death by vomit and shaken me into looking at myself properly. He wasn't so vile, as older brothers went.

'Are you looking forward to university?' I asked, perching myself on his beanbag.

'Yeah, if I get in.'

'You will if you pull your finger out.'

'Thanks.'

'Patchouli thinks it's all a waste of time, that you just end up in a burger bar like everyone else.'

'Maybe so,' Chris conceded, 'but that's beside the point. I'll have had three years' experience of studying a subject I really want to study, meeting people I wouldn't meet anywhere else, freedom from all the work ethic hassle plus half-price entry to all the best gigs.'

'And getting away from home.'

'Yeah—that's how it should be. I've got the rest of my life to worry about stuff like mortgages and jobs.'

'Sounds like a degree just postpones all that for three years.'

'As well as giving you choices you wouldn't otherwise have.'

'Like which burger bar you work in?' I asked.

He propped himself up on one elbow, taking my quip seriously. 'No, like how long you choose to stay in the burger bar. Unemployment rates for graduates are still pretty low—less than six per cent in my subject. I'll take those odds.'

'You've changed your tune.'

'Only because I've found out the hard way that what Mum says makes sense. Listen, Sue, I was hanging around with kids like Patchouli last year and I've got sod all to show for it. I know not everybody needs to go to uni to be successful but when you're like us, where "Daddy" can't just slip you twenty grand to set you up in business, you need all the choices you can get.'

I nodded shyly in agreement. I preferred Chris's vision of my educational future to Patchouli's and I'd tell her so next time I saw her. 'I think you'll definitely pass Sociology this time, Chris,' I grinned.

'I know I will. Don't tell the Maid of Scutari though or she'll only find something else to nag me about.'

'Like cleaning your room,' I said, eyeing the plate of half eaten sandwiches and the socks scattered like cotton worm-casts under his bed. He responded with a loud belch which almost drowned out the phone ringing downstairs. We both raced to answer it, screaming dementedly and pretending to throw punches at each other as we collided down the steps. I got there first, pushing big bro's hand out of the way and laughing my head off as he fell backwards into the table and sent everything flying. 'Hello?' I said into the receiver as Chris effed his way through the piles of old bills and *Yellow Pages* while Mum shouted at him to mind his language.

'Sounds like there's a war going on,' Tina stated.

'Oh,' I said, surprised to hear her voice.

'Can you do me a favour, Suzanne? Candy can't do Wednesday afternoon for me. Could you be an angel and cover after school until half-five with Karenna? I've got my old ladies and they get upset if I don't turn up.'

She paused, waiting for my answer. I had two career choices, yes or no. 'Yes,' I said, 'no problem.'

'Lovely. Thanks a lot, love.'

'My pleasure.'

James Dean was barely civil as I lay in bed, trying to interest him in all my news. 'Thought I was just a poster to you now?'

'You are, but we can still be friends,' I cajoled.

'Don't string me that old line.'

'I thought about you dying today—it made me cry.'

'What for? Best thing I did: die young, leave a pretty corpse, that's my motto. Hell, look at Brando—the guy is obese. Who wants to wind up like that?'

'He stands up for what he believes in, though—rights for native Americans and . . . '

'The guy's an asshole—always was, always will be. "I could've been a contender." Bull.'

I stared into the soft darkness. 'Did you ever have a moment in your life when everything changed? When you knew nothing would ever be the same again?'

'Sure.'

'When?'

'September 20, 1955, 5.58 p.m. Highway 41.'

'The day you died.'

'My beautiful Porsche . . . '

'Mine was today on the way home from school.'

'What happened?'

'I got my life back.'

14

Tina had just completed loading plastic boxes of hairdressing equipment into the back of her car when I arrived outside the salon. 'Oh, Suzanne, you're here,' she greeted, a relieved smile on her lips.

'Been busy?' I asked conversationally.

My boss glanced across the street, then banged down her hatchback with a firm 'thwack'. 'No, it's been dead all day. Listen, if Bernie Sheldon, Karenna's dad comes in . . . '

'Yes?'

She hesitated before declining to elaborate. 'Oh, nothing. I overreact sometimes. Here, before I forget . . . ' From her purse, Tina extracted a twenty pound note and handed it to me. 'Overtime,' she explained, noticing my puzzled expression. It was a generous amount for two hours and I began to suspect her motives for my windfall.

'Thanks,' I muttered, burying it deep into my school trousers. I had a feeling I was going to earn it.

She patted my arm, then waited until a lorry passed before walking to her car door. 'See you,' she waved and left me to it. Inside, I gave Karenna a cold smile and headed for the staffroom to dump my bag.

Behind the teak cladding, I did my breathing exercises, knowing they would calm me, stop me from showing how nervous I was. I had been in training since Tina's phone call. From my bag I pulled out a tight-fitting sweater I had bought in the sales but never worn. I knew I looked good in it and it helped to boost my confidence as I slid it over my head. I glanced in the mirror opposite, forcing myself to smile.

I had re-read Steetley's handbook on bullying, memorizing the advice it gives on being assertive. Look cool. Walk tall. Act confident. Maintain eye contact. Don't accept put-downs. Challenge the bully's actions. Question verbal insults. Today was my showdown, and I was totally focused.

When I returned to the salon, I walked unhurriedly to the window display, immediately busying myself. At the same moment, two women pushed open the salon door. 'Is it still student night on Wednesdays?' one of them enquired.

'Yes,' Karenna smiled, ever-attentive.

They came in, buoyant and giddy. Karenna totally monopolized them, feeding them questions and compliments. I might as well have been invisible. She barely spoke to me during the next hour and a half as a steady trickle of students wanting the most for their cheap-rate haircuts flitted in and out. Some were loud and over-confident, others unassuming and ordinary. It was interesting to see Karenna treating them all with an undeserved reverence. 'I suppose you'll be like them soon,' she sniffed as the last one breezed out.

'What do you mean?' I asked, gathering towels she had just ordered me to take to The Wash Tub.

'Full of yourself, thinking you're a cut above.'

'I don't think so,' I replied coolly, dumping the stale, damp linens into a basket. 'How much will I need for the machines?'

She glanced at me. I met her gaze full-on, not as the usual rabbit caught in headlights, but as the knight beholding the dragon. 'You're very cocky all of a sudden,' she said, moving across to the till.

'Am I?' I asked.

'You usually wet yourself when I come near you.'

It was the first time Karenna had actually admitted

out loud any such history between us. I wasn't going to let it pass. 'Oh, you remember now, do you? I thought you'd forgotten.'

A cruel smile flitted across her lips. 'You were my favourite, Fishy. Such easy bait.'

'I know,' I replied, 'I was pathetic, as you often said.'

She sniggered, pushing an assortment of coins into my hand. 'At least you admit it. Do you remember that time I forced you to eat Fiona's ham sarnie?' she asked confidingly.

I stared at her in astonishment, hardly able to believe her gall. 'I'll go do these,' I said, blanking her.

'Don't be long, just dump them in the machine, then come back,' she ordered tersely.

There was only one washing machine available in the launderette. I stuffed the towels into the opening, then realized I hadn't got any powder. The dispenser was, naturally, out of order, so I strolled back to Snippits. 'Have we got any—' I began, stopping mid-sentence when I saw the look on Karenna's face.

It was grey and bloodless, her eyes focused somewhere beyond my head. I twisted round, startled to find a man slouched against the picture window, hands pressed against the glass pane.

The bloke was tall but gaunt, his wasted body making little impression inside the dark suit he was wearing. I knew he must be Bernie Sheldon, Karenna's dad. She had his features, although what must once have been a good-looking face, like hers, had self-destructed. From the glazed but darting eyes which buzzed from me to Karenna, I knew drugs, not nature, etched his skin now. 'What do you want?' she snarled at him, yet keeping her distance like a cornered rat.

For a second, he looked as if he would slide all the way down the glass but her question mobilized him. Slowly, he stood up, making his way falteringly towards her. He ignored me totally and I watched, full of curiosity, as he held his arms out to embrace her. The movement released a smell of rank telephone boxes and rancid beer. 'Renna, Renna,' he mumbled.

Karenna fled to the other side of the reception desk, jabbing a steel comb in the air between them. 'Get away, you bastard!' she shouted, her voice high-pitched, almost a squeal.

The man dropped his arms and shook his head from side to side. 'Tuh! Did you hear that?' Robotically, he turned to me. 'Did you hear that? Would you talk to your dad like that? Would you?'

I didn't respond. My mute reply seemed to please the greaseball. 'No, she wouldn't, see. She wouldn't talk to her daddy like that.'

Shuffling on his unsteady feet, he advanced slightly towards the desk. The movement was small but deliberate and sly. It reminded me of when kids play 'What time is it, Mr Wolf' but Karenna hadn't noticed. 'Get away!' she repeated.

'I just want to talk to you, princess. I can talk to my own daughter, can't I? My little girl?'

Bernie Sheldon made my skin crawl. Even though he had used the same endearment my dad used with me, I could not imagine what it must have been like having this specimen as a father. He made another barely perceptible movement towards Karenna but she seemed frozen. 'What do you want?' she asked, her voice almost a whisper.

I felt my insides shrivel like melted cling-film as I recognized the fear Karenna was feeling. I knew it so well. She was terrified.

Suddenly, her dad leapt forward and gave her a swift, vicious flick with his thumb and forefinger which landed in the hollow of her cheek. My hand automatically flew to my own face where I nursed an imaginary wound. I relived the pain exactly, from the initial sting, to the numbness, then finally the throbbing, as if the cheekbone were about to explode.

The Sheldon finger-flick. A tradition passed down

through the generations, happily shared by all. What a revelation.

I'd worked out a long time ago that there had to be a reason for Karenna's behaviour. Nobody can be so cruel without being taught how. No doubt somewhere along the line, someone had been equally cruel and damaging to her father. But damaged children pass damage on and they had made me part of their nightmarish lives without giving a toss for the consequences. Whatever the reason for their bleak existence, I didn't see why I should have had to pay for it, either in the past or now.

I resented being here, tricked into witnessing this ugly relationship. I told myself none of this had anything to do with me and I ought to just leave them to it.

The junkie's eyes darted to the till, then to me. 'You won't say owt, if she borrows some, will you? That cow Lockwood's rolling in it. I bet you could do with a bit extra, couldn't you? Buy a CD or summat.' The guy actually beamed at me, the deadly smile of the snake-charmer.

The urge to leave disappeared immediately. He was not going to draw me into this. 'You'd better go,' I said, 'or I'll call the police.'

He seemed amused. 'Call away, gorgeous. She'll not say owt if you do.'

I glanced across at Karenna and saw it was true. Like a battered wife, she would hate every inch of him but defend him to the hilt in front of others. That was how they got away with it. Again, he advanced.

'Just a fiver, Karenna, duck. Just to see me through the night. I won't bother you again, I promise.' His eyes filled with ready tears.

Karenna shook her head pitifully. 'I told you, I've nothing left. I gave you all I had last week.'

'You can have this,' I said, placing the twenty quid Tina had given me on the counter.

Bernie Sheldon stared at me, briefly puzzled by my action, before greedily pocketing the note. 'Thanks, duck,' he said, his tears suddenly drying. 'I 'preciate it.' Without another word he stumbled out, leaving a lingering stench to remind us of his presence.

I didn't stop shaking until twenty minutes after he'd gone, despite locking the salon up and flicking the sign on to 'closed'. The towels in The Wash Tub would have to fend for themselves.

Karenna was slumped on one of the leatherette seats in the staffroom, puffing out cigarette smoke in short, stabbing bursts. The dragon in its death throes.

Even now she was unyielding. 'What are you staring at, you slag?' she challenged as I asked if she wanted a coffee.

I saw her words for what they were—empty attempts at bravado. 'I just came in to see if you were all right,' I said.

'What do you care? I bet you're loving all this, aren't you?'

'No, I'm not. I feel sorry for you.'

'Don't waste your pity on me, kid. I don't need it— from you or anybody else.'

I leaned against the sink, staring down at her in her defeat, as I had done so often in my dreams. Only this time it was real. I had no intention of seeing her again after today—what was the point of churning myself up every Saturday, reliving the past every time I looked at her? But I couldn't go without her realizing what she had done to me. It was important she knew, to close the circle. 'I used to have nightmares because of you,' I disclosed.

Her response was typically hard and arrogant. 'So bloody what?'

'You terrified me for two years. If you hadn't left when you did I think I'd have had a breakdown.'

She sniggered. Without her posh clients around, and her surrogate mother Tina to impress, the real Sheldon could re-emerge in all her glory. 'Big chuffing deal. You shouldn't have took it then, should you? We weren't the fucking mafia. Listen, I've got more to worry about than your skinny hide, so don't start giving me all this guilt crap. How do you think I feel, seeing you here?'

'What do you mean?'

Karenna's eyes flashed moistly at me. 'Here! In my place, staring at me with those little cow eyes of yours, unnerving me.'

I saw instantly how my presence here threatened her in the new world she had created for herself. I was a reminder of the shabby adolescence she had so far hidden from those who only knew the reinvented model. How could she fawn over clients like Nicky Pattinson when I was only inches away, a loose cannon who might shoot her mouth off with grubby anecdotes any second? With a jolt I realized she was as scared of me as I was of her—but she had more to lose. Knowing this didn't give me any sense of triumph. Instead, I tried to offer advice.

'You know Tina won't put up with your dad forever. Even in a Sweaty Betty's,' I said, repeating Patchouli's derogatory term for the salon. 'Nobody will, no matter how brilliant you are at dyeing hair. You'll never get beyond junior stylist.'

This obviously hit a nerve. 'So what do you suggest, know-all?'

'You'll have to stand up to him.'

Karenna fumbled in her bag for another cigarette. 'Have you ever stood up to a drug addict?' she asked, her voice cold and empty.

'No.'

'So do me a favour—stop patronizing me and grow up.'

I shrugged. Karenna might be good at cutting hair but she was rubbish at observing human behaviour. I had grown up.

She watched in silence as I pulled my Steetley sweatshirt over my head. 'Where are you off?' she asked.

'Home. I agreed to work till half five and it's gone that,' I replied curtly.

Karenna reached up, tightening her fingers round my arm. 'We haven't finished yet—there's the sinks to clean and the towels to fetch . . . '

I shook her hand away. 'I've kept my part of the bargain. I'm going.' I picked up my bag and headed towards the main door. She followed restlessly, arms folded across her chest.

'What did you give him your money for?' she asked hoarsely.

'To pay you back,' I said.

'How do you work that one out?' she sneered.

'It was Tina's conscience money for me staying with you today. I didn't want it—I'm not taking any of you with me when I go.' I reached the door, prised back the lock, then paused. 'All you had to do was say sorry.'

'For what?' she asked.

'For your own sake.'

She glared at me with her poisoned eyes but I was immune. I'd got rid of her. Not from my mind—the scars from those two years would take a long time to heal—but from my heart. I was whole.

Tina drove up just as I was leaving. I waited as she wound down her window. 'Everything go off all right?' she asked.

'Sort of,' I replied.

'Lovely, see you Saturday.'

'Can't do it, sorry.'

'Oh?'

'It's not my thing, hairdressing.'

'Well, it's a bit short notice.'

'Say goodbye to Candy for me,' I asked.

Tina didn't answer. I was already just one of the flighty girls who used to work for her. Inside, I could see Karenna scrubbing diligently around the sinks as if she'd been at it for hours.

A few metres ahead, a 59 bus groaned to a halt in the lay-by. I dashed up to it, clattering on to the platform like an eager bride waiting to be chased upstairs. 'Where to, chuck?' the driver asked.

'Home,' I said, smiling.

Other books by Helena Pielichaty

Vicious Circle
ISBN 0 19 271775 8

'Why haven't we got any money? We've never got any money. Why can't we be like other people and have fish and chips when we fancy?'

Ten-year-old Louisa May and her mother Georgette are two of the 'have-nots', shuttling between ever-seedier bed and breakfast accommodation. To help cope with this way of life they play elaborate fantasy games, pretending to be the characters in the romantic fiction that Georgette borrows from the library in every town they move to.

When they arrive at the Cliff Top Villas Hotel in a run-down seaside resort and Georgette falls ill, it looks as if the fantasy will have to end. But Louisa May enlists the help of Joanna, another hotel resident, and together they determine to find out the truth behind Georgette's 'let's pretend' existence. Maybe this way there will be a chance for them to break out of the vicious circle and become 'haves' at last . . .

'The story is told with a strong sense of humour and is highly readable.'

Newark Advertiser

Simone's Letters
ISBN 0 19 271816 9

*Dear Mr Cakebread . . . For starters my name is Simone, not
Simon . . . Mum says you sound just like my dad. My dad,
Dennis, lives in Bartock with his girlfriend, Alexis . . . My mum
says lots of rude things about her because Alexis was one of the
reasons my parents got divorced (I was the other) . . .*

When ten-year-old Simone starts writing letters to Jem
Cakebread, the leading man of a touring theatre company,
she begins a friendship that will change her life . . . and the
lives of all around her: her mum, her best friend Chloe, her
new friend Melanie—and not forgetting Jem himself!

This collection of funny and often touching letters charts
Simone's final year at Primary School; from a school visit to
Rumpelstiltskin's Revenge to her final leaving Assembly;
through the ups and downs of her friendships—and those
of her mum and dad.

River Boy
Tim Bowler
ISBN 0 19 275035 6
Winner of the 1998 Carnegie Medal

Grandpa is dying. He can barely move his hands any more but, stubborn as ever, refuses to stay in hospital. He's determined to finish one last painting before he goes.

At first Jess can't understand his refusal to let go, but then she too becomes involved in the mysterious painting. And when she meets the river boy himself, she finds she is suddenly caught up in a challenge of her own that she must complete—before it's too late . . .

Dark Thread
Pauline Chandler
ISBN 0 19 271761 8

'I thought I saw someone,' Kate murmured, shaking her head. She wondered if she was going mad.

'This place is full of ghosts,' the woman said, lightly.

Kate knows the mill well. She and her mother had an exhibition of their weaving there. Before.

But that was a different life, before the accident. And now Kate knows that she just can't cope any more.

But when she suddenly finds herself back in another world that is strange and familiar all at the same time, Kate finds that she has no choice. She has to keep going, to survive, and to protect the other people in her new family. This new way of life is exhausting and unrelenting. And in the background there is always the mill, with the machines that never stop, the work which never ends, and the dangerous power that drives it.

Facing the Dark
Michael Harrison
ISBN 0 19 271801 0

Everything had changed the moment I opened the door to the two men. It was worse, somehow, that I had been the one to let them in, the one who ended our family life.

Simon's father has been accused of the murder of a rival cab driver and Simon faces a life branded as the son of a murderer. Then he meets Charley, grieving for her dead father, the murder victim, and they determine to find out the real story behind the murder.

An exciting thriller of two young people, trying to find out the truth behind a murder—but menaced by an unseen danger.

Walking the Maze
Margret Shaw
ISBN 0 19 271754 5

Stories can be dangerous, and so can imagination. Annice has too much of both.

She doesn't realize the danger at first. Not until it's too late. She is sucked into a story, into the world of a painting, which becomes more real to her than real life. Like sleepwalking, like fantasy, she becomes part of people's lives until she no longer knows what is real and what isn't. Walking the maze will lead to tragedy. But which is the way out?